The Treatments

When the time came we walked singing to the clinic, and Paul left me for a week while they bombarded my body and brain with chemicals, rays and spirits, trying to blast the mortality from me in ways which were then great mysteries, and which I have since studied at desperate length, to no avail. Paul was waiting for me when I left the clinic, and we capered about the Himalayas, watched the sun set over the Rockies and the moon rise from the Pyrenees, spent ecstatic ages in the underwater city of Venice. A year later, I returned to the clinic for the rest of the treatments, and they kept me there, and tested, and tested and finally told me that it hadn't worked.

At all.

Books by Marta Randall

Islands
Journey

Published by POCKET BOOKS

MARTA RANDALL

ISLANDS

PUBLISHED BY POCKET BOOKS NEW YORK

Earlier version of the work was previously published
by Pyramid/Jove Books.

POCKET BOOKS, a Simon & Schuster division of
GULF & WESTERN CORPORATION
1230 Avenue of the Americas, New York, N.Y. 10020

ISBN: 0-671-83411-8

First Pocket Books printing May, 1980

10 9 8 7 6 5 4 3 2 1

POCKET and colophon are trademarks of Simon & Schuster.

Printed in the U.S.A.

for
three Richards
one Nell
and
a Margaret
with love

1

Far below me the invisible surf smashed repeatedly against the equally invisible rocks, ebbing with a vast, sucking rush over the stones. The night wind was cold, as cold as the frigid stars or the icy pallor of the moon as it broke through the clouds and cast a dim, diffused glow across the sea. Deep in the base of my spine, something twinged and nagged and sent out a quick, exploratory shaft of pain. I gripped the textured redwood of the rail with both hands and willed the numbness of my feet to move in a straight line through me, up to my back and heart and mind, chilling them. But I could coax the coldness only as far as my knees before it ebbed again. I tipped my head far back, body arching toward the sky, and the pain blossomed.

Two stories below me Paul and Jenny, curled around each other in the large transparent bed, made love quietly, so that I, presumably in the room just below them, would not hear. Considerate of them. The sounds of Paul's lovemaking would be too much to

take; had been too much, when I heard them briefly
on my way to the roof balcony; the small gasps of
pleasure pursuing me as I fled up the stairs, the
explosively gentle sound of Paul in orgasm. Still the
same, that sound, after all the years. Remembering, I
clung more tightly to the rail until the pain lessened
and I could breathe again. It was a mistake to invite
them here, I told myself fiercely. Stupid to think that
it wouldn't bother me, stupid to think that I was over
it, over wanting at all. Idiocy, and I am well punished
for it.

I drank the cold air until the shaking stopped and
the pain retreated to a small reminder buried in me.
I freed my hands from the rails and slipped quietly
down the spiral stairs, past the murky glow of the
stained-glass windows, past the landing by the guest
room door. I closed and locked my door behind me,
thumbed on the lights, and my reflection leaped out at
me from the large, dark window. Oh, let's look, yes,
at Tia in the flesh, the drug-resisting meat. Tia the
anomaly, the freak. Withered, by all means; flat stomach crossed again and again by lines, breasts hanging
low but never large enough to make much difference;
ass wrinkled, thighs sinewy and shrunken, calves the
same; skinny arms ending in big, square, capable
hands. Face weathered around brown eyes, skin dried
and lined as driftwood, hair streaked with grey and
dry from constant exposure to the sun. Dry lady,
driftwood hag. Well, if I must age, then let me not
disguise it—no creams, plastic surgeries, cosmetics.
Let them be uncomfortable at the sight of Tia Hamley,
growing ungracefully old in a world of the forever
young.

And let them never guess her to be unexpectedly
tortured by the thought of her former lover lying in
the guest room, serpented around his latest lady. Let
it be a secret between me, and the window, and the
beast at the base of my spine. Hush.

2

Fifty years ago he was my lover, when I was seventeen and he twenty-seven. He was easy in his youth, looking as he does now: grey-green eyes muted to hazel brown in the evenings; long gold and brown hair swept around a strong-boned face; a slight build, narrow about the shoulders and hips; quick in his movements, in his words. A good, pleasing body, and he had not opted to have it changed.

And I? Portrait of the freak as a young girl? Rounded and firm, masses of auburn hair constantly falling into brown eyes, 1.6 meters tall, almost as tall as Paul. I remember the child as laughing, sparkling, singing in her chains like the sea. I was, quite literally, poised on the brink of eternity, waiting for my body to stabilize enough to take the Immortality Treatments, and Paul was still exulting in the newness of his own immortality.

When the time came we walked singing to the clinic, and Paul left me for a week while they bombarded my body and brain with chemicals, rays, and spirits,

trying to blast the mortality from me in ways which
were then great mysteries to me, and which I have
since studied at desperate length, to no avail. Paul
was waiting for me when I left the clinic, and we
capered about the Himalayas, watched the sun set
over the Rockies and the moon rise from the Pyrenees,
spent ecstatic ages in the underwater city of Venice.
A year later I returned to the clinic for the rest of the
treatments, and they kept me there, and tested, and
tested, and finally told me that it hadn't worked.

At all.

I would live a long time, yes, they would see to it.
Not forever, no, we're terribly sorry. You're unique,
you know. Maybe one hundred, maybe one hundred
and fifty years. We're sorry.

Maybe two hundred. It's not so bad, to live two
hundred years. You'll live quite well, you know.
We'll see to it. We'll pay you for it; we need you. As
much as you need us.

You'll live very well.

But not youthfully.

So sorry.

So after a while I went away sterile and lived on
the moon, spent years alone in the station orbiting the
sun, lived on Mars, and came back middle-aged to
a world of the young. Went away again, to Saturn, to
Venus, kept lonely outposts in nightmarish places.
Came back ancient and bought my house at the end
of the continent, worked on the project, and immersed
myself in the convoluted involvement of dredging
the ocean bottom for the past. Accepted Paul and his
lady into my home, recognized the shock in his eyes
as they disembarked from the cruiser and I stepped
forward to meet them: "This is the woman I slept
with, so many years ago?"

No, I told him in my mind. No, she's gone, she of
the sleek round body and auburn hair. I'm just bor-
rowing her name.

3

I used to go for days on end without considering the fact that they would probably never let me die. After all, they needed me, those of them who specialized in the archaic art of gerontology. There would be, they thought, no others like me; they had guaranteed that I would produce no others myself. Of course they would not let me go. So I would be left to grow older and older, drying with age until I became a grasshopper caged in some kind institution's basement, amid the wires and machines; a legend used to threaten our few children into obedience. Nightmare stuff. True enough. I should practice for my part, take up drooling at odd hours of the day, or pace around the *Ilium*'s decks shouting nonsense. But most of my colleagues were terrified enough of me already, even those fifty or one hundred and fifty years older than I. They looked at me with awe, they thought I possessed great wisdom, merely because my body withered perceptibly around me.

Many years before, wandering slightly dazed and

miserable through the library at Luna, I had enter-
tained a pleasant fantasy. Again I would enter the
Treatment Center in southern Africa, a smiling at-
tendant would touch a hidden button and an image
would form in the middle of the room. An image of a
bronzed and laughing woman, firm and youthful. And,
my payment of suffering completed, I would be allowed to become that woman again. Gazing at my
reflection in the darkened window, that first night of
Paul's visit, I remembered the silly, seductive illusion
of my youth, smiled grimly at the actual image, and
prepared for sleep.

4

Paul awakened early and came out to where I puttered around my sand garden, needlessly cultivating the tough beach grasses. He brought me a cup of coffee and I stopped work to talk with him.

No, he hadn't changed at all. He sprawled over the stone bench, naked and at ease in the morning breezes. I, of course, was clothed; it was as much a source of wonderment to my colleagues as my greying hair and withered face. I glanced at Paul's body quickly before lowering my gaze to my archaic stoneware cup, and we talked about our found Atlantis.

"No, you've got your legends confused," I told him. "It's Hawaii, some parts of the islands that sank during the Great Shaping. Interesting, yes, but not Atlantis."

Paul shrugged and smiled. What did he know of Atlantis? "And you are looking for . . ."

Youth, I was tempted to tell him. The Fountain of Immortality, the Philosopher's Stone, to transmute lead to gold. Or bronze.

"Anything," I said. "Houses, any papers that might have survived, artwork. Sometimes we find old safes, watertight, full of papers and other perishables. Machines, materials, jewelry, bits and pieces of other people's lives."

He looked appreciative. He had to, of course. He and Jenny were spending quite a bit to work with us for three months, under the blankets of the sea.

"What have you found?"

"This and that. You'll see most of it later this morning, when you go down to the ship. It's not much, yet, and it hasn't really been systematized, but it'll give you a fairly good idea of what we'll be looking for once we go under."

He nodded, still smiling, and his unwavering gaze disturbed me. I looked away from him, out over the edge of the cliff toward the waters. The mainland was a fuzz on the horizon, and the clouds of the night before had disappeared with the dawn, leaving the air infinitely blue and infinitely clean. Far out, seabirds hovered and swept, their calls coming faintly to me over the waves.

"And you, Tia?"

"Um?"

"How have you been? It's been a long time."

"Yes, it has," I said abruptly. "I've been well, thank you. Is Jenny up? It's time for breakfast and I should get you to the dock early. Tobias will be waiting."

"I'll see," he replied, stood, stretched, and loped toward the house.

I resisted watching him and bent instead to my plants. How had I been, indeed. How had he expected me to have been? Was this young Immortal mocking me? Playing games with my emotions?

Or only being polite?

Or all of the above, or none of the above, or Tia you are becoming paranoid. I left my garden and went into the house to prepare breakfast.

5

I do not like my kitchen. I tried to hide the equipment when I reconstructed the room, but it still intruded, the storage units and recall units and heaters standing out in alien bleakness against the solemnity of my home. The house speaks to me; it too grows old beyond its time, it too contains modern intrusions, just as I contain bits of pipe and plastic, replacements and repairs.

I discovered the house sitting derelict, askew, when I first joined the project and began looking for somewhere other than aboard the *Ilium* to live. The house was ancient, pre-Shaping, made from the wood of the now extinct redwood. Constructed in a series of cubes and rectangles, it perched precariously on the edge of a cliff and spilled over to hang suspended above the surf. That it had not disappeared ages ago was the work of some Immortal who had shored the building haphazardly with a collection of forcefields and ugly plasteel stilts, then abandoned it when it no longer served his purpose. Its ability to sustain the depredations of both time and incompetent repairs, more than anything else, had endeared it to me. I traced the owner, who was then running a brothel in Gagarin, and after some trouble reminding him that the house belonged to him, I succeeded in buying it.

I also bought the land for two square kilometers around the house, and spent the majority of my time between voyages rebuilding. I had new foundations put in, reanchored the house firmly in place, removed the hideous struts. Contracted with a firm in Africa specializing in rare and extinct woods, and they came up with something close enough to the original redwood to fool an expert. I jigsawed, tucked, gathered and nipped until the house was in as near its original shape as possible. I bought old pots and filled them with plants, I covered some of the windows with heavy drapes and others with antique polarized glass; had weavers make me rugs from ancient patterns, bought solid sculpture and old paintings.

No one likes it but me, naturally. The walls are fixed in place, won't flow and move at one's least command; they are certain, stable, solid, good. The furniture is furniture, not invisible forcefields that mold themselves to your every contour. You have to make some concessions to my furniture, you have to compromise, reach an agreement with it. My bed will not turn into a table for you, nor will my fireplace (yes, a real fireplace, and I burn real wood in it with real fire) become a chair. Solid, as I am. Firmly rooted in the reality of its own existence.

It's all a front, of course. Turn my house into a version of my own monstrosity and convince myself that freakery is a great and good thing. Still, it helps, and who am I to refuse the comforts of self-deception?

6

They had wanted me to stay at the clinic after the second useless try at the Immortality Treatments, wanted me to be where they could conveniently poke and pry and test, but I wouldn't stay and they couldn't make me, although, at one point, they threatened to call me before the claims and adjudication council in Berne. But the Law reads, simply, that "No person shall damage or defraud, or cause to be damaged or defrauded, any other person," and that's it. There was no possible way they could twist that around to force me to stay as the sole occupant of their new zoo. So I left, very quickly, before Paul could be notified, and wandered about the face of the earth. Four days in Istanbul, eight days in Australia, two days in Beijing, one week in the quiet seashore city of Diablo, gazing east from the island across the California Sea to the Sierras, gazing west beyond Tam Island at the Pacific Ocean. Paul found me there and again I fled, so far north that north ran out and I sat at the top of the globe, shivering in the heat of the large hotel. I wandered the fringes of the arctic, watched the aurora streak and curtain across the darkening sky. Spent time below the surface of the snows, down in the echoing Caverns of Ice.

"As you will note," said the guide, motioning from the floating platform at the curving walls around us, "the initial melt was deceptive. The Ancients laid their cables in a great grid under the arctic ice, using submarines to guide the initial operations and primitive remotes to do the actual placement. When the grid was completed, they began warming the ice, from here, below. The theory, it seems, was that since the inner portions of the ice mass would melt more slowly, the heat needed to keep them in pace with the outer sections would be correspondingly greater. It would have made more sense, of course, to grid and melt the outer sections first, floating the floes down the ocean currents to various locations where they would be used to provide water for the cities and croplands. However, records tell us that the Ancients were unwilling to do so; each country refused to let any other country have its ice first, and in their greed and haste and fear they attempted to provide for all simultaneously." The guide paused. "Imagine it, then: a vision of the cap suddenly divided into a checkerboard, and each piece towed down the walls of the world. Unfortunately, it didn't work. The thermostatic controls for the inner sections were set much too high, causing the ice to melt, heat, boil, melt more ice, until the entire core of the ice mass liquified. Ocean levels rose steadily as the melt escaped below the ice mass into the waters below; more catastrophically, a confined amount of melt broke through what were, by then, the thin edges of the ice mass, and sent great swells moving south. Instead of life-giving icefloes, the Ancients generated death-giving floods." The guide shrugged, as though one could hardly have expected better of parties who were not, after all, immortal.

The floating platform stopped before a wall of layered ice, clean and fresh toward the bottom, increasingly dirty as we rose, and broken by bands almost black with pollution near the top. My attention drifted and, as I was feeling sorry for myself, I wondered how many layers of ice would form during the ageless lifetimes of the Immortals who shared the hovering platform with me. They jostled close to the edge, peering at the grime. I moved away from them and stared down at the bleak bottom of the cavern, imagined it bursting with boiling water, shivered, and turned to the guide again.

"Much of the upheaval of the Great Shaping is directly attributable to the flooding, but various geologic reactions caused even more damage. The sudden lack of pressure at the pole caused shifting in the earth's tectonic plates, resulting in earthquakes and volcanic upheavals far beyond anything recorded in history. Crowded conditions and the decline of fossil fuels had prompted the Ancients to build nuclear power plants in haste and without necessary precautions, and many of these were located along fault lines and other areas where the full force of the Shaping was felt. Here, on our left, is a hologrammatic representation of the line of volcanic and radioactive activity during the decades following . . ."

My attention wandered again. I had come to the Caverns hoping to solace the small tragedy of my own life with the greater tragedy of the past, but found no comfort. My fellow tourists, it was apparent, found more of interest in the machinery of destruction than in the human tragedy of it. I stood away from them and spent the remainder of the tour staring down at the frigid wonders below.

When we emerged into the lobby of the hotel, the familiar and unwelcome figure of Paul approached me, would not let me escape. We argued violently and at length, *sotto voce* in the crowded restaurant, in hisses and whispers in the bars, in screams and shouts at the door to my room where I would not let him enter. As the worried guards appeared to calm the uproar, I fled again, out of the hotel, into a hastily rented hopper and far from him and his pleas that I be content to spend the remainder of my brief time gratefully growing ugly in the shelter of his arms. I knew even as I fled that it was not Paul I evaded, but the knowledge of what I could have been, the knowledge of what I had expected to be during the time we had shared our lives. As I flew over the swept coldness, I remembered the flecked worry in his eyes. And hated myself for weeping.

7

I liked the Jenny-creature. An unforeseen development, which I pondered over breakfast. She moved with grace, unselfconsciously, slipping an occasional comment into the conversation that was sharp, to the point, and often quite funny. But for the most part she kept her peace, watching Paul and me with her quiet green eyes. She wasn't pretty, really, hadn't opted for cosmetic surgery, so that her nose was a bit too big, a bit too sharp; her high, fine and out-of-fashion cheekbones rode above concave cheeks, and a tumult of black hair fell over her shoulders. I liked her, and the liking surprised me.

She was bothered by me, though, by my obvious age, my abruptness, my murmured sarcasms as I drove them in my ancient electric hover-car down the steep dirt roads to the dock. Did she know of my history with Paul? For that matter, did Paul really know anymore, did he remember Venice, or was it a vague piece of knowledge tucked into the back of his mind and forgotten? After all, it couldn't have been too pleasant, looking at my aging self and recollecting our brief passion, eons back. Did it even matter?

Yes. To me.

8

They were both terrified of the hover-car and of my driving, and I knew that they would be. Paul sat clutching the arm-rest on the passenger side and Jenny was sandwiched between us, clutching Paul, as I swung the little car around the steep curves of the road. Perfectly safe, that road and my driving of it; I knew every small bend and switchback, every place where water accumulated during rainfalls and where dried leaves fell in autumn. The road and the land through which it passed were beautiful, but my passengers were so bound up in their fear that they did not sense the beauty, and I found myself once again exasperated by the typical, infuriating terror of the Immortals. I deliberately speeded up, took the curves with greater bravado; if they insisted on fright, at least let their fears be well founded. The little car squealed and skidded. I forgot my sarcasms and concentrated on control, feeling the flight between my hands, the sharp rocking as the aircushions below encountered unevenness, the wind through my hair. I

must have looked the maniac, grinning into the wind,
for Paul and Jenny were pale and stiff as we rounded
the last swing but one in the road, and I suddenly re-
versed thrust and pulled over.

"There she is," I said, gesturing out toward the sea.
They came out of their terror slowly, followed the line
of my arm, saw the *Ilium*, and gasped.

Imagine an iceberg, pointed at bow and stern,
broad along its midsection, rising straight and clean
from waterline to decks. Below the waterline, unseen,
the hull flares to cover the antigrav housing, the generators, beamers, all the apparatus of movement and
of flight. But the decks are an ice-dream carved by a
sculptor with an overactive imagination. The *Ilium*
is a broad-beamed cathedral of a ship, spired and
buttressed, castellated, crystalline; a floating opera, a
palace, a folly. Three hundred years of Immortal tin-
kering had turned her from a plain, white grav-
schooner to an illustration from an ancient, fantastical
story book, and only the boundaries of her hull limited
the fantasy of her decks. The morning sunlight shattered against windows and metal arches, poured
down smooth sides and bounced from intricate ones,
picking out an arched and colored window here, a
minaret there, a series of wrought-iron balconies.
Staircases spiraled endlessly; colonnades appeared
unexpectedly and just as unexpectedly disappeared;
flags of many hues rippled from the top of each tower,
turret, minaret, and spire. The *Ilium* flew her gaudy
colors proudly as she sat scrubbed and gleaming a
kilometer from the shore. My passengers stared,
open-mouthed, and in thanks for their awe I drove
very slowly and carefully the remaining kilometer to
the dock.

I stopped the rotor. They silently clambered from
the car and stood holding each other and gazing at the
ship while Tobias, slouched against the metal arch
of the dock's entrance, pulled himself upright and
came toward us. He stopped a yard away and, leav-

ing Paul and Jenny to their awe, he scowled at me. I returned the courtesy.

Beautiful Tobias. Mass of curly, golden hair, Grecian-perfect face, eyes an intense blue. Tanned, graceful, sensuous. When clothed, and he was clothed surprisingly often for an Immortal, he wore ragged pants, grease-stained suits, as though he thought the contrast heightened his own beauty. Which, of course, it did. Tobias hated me. Perhaps I was too great a contrast, perhaps I reminded him of the mutability which should have been his lot. For whatever reason, Tobias hated me and I found the hate refreshingly unlike the polite, uneasy masks of the other Immortals. I suspected that if Tobias knew my appreciation of his dislike, he would stop immediately, and I had no intention of allowing that to pass. So we silently reaffirmed our mutual aversion, standing there in the hot July sunlight beside the wonder-struck novices, and he dropped his glance first.

"Are you coming out to the ship," he demanded, staring over my left shoulder.

"No, I'm busy today. I'll be down on time tomorrow morning. Am I needed?"

"Not at all," he replied, and smiled like a sullen child in on some secret. He knew damned well that today was my regular reaming-out day. I turned from him in disgust and called to Paul and Jenny.

"This is Tobias Gamin, he'll take you out to the *Ilium* and show you around, introduce you to people. Tobias, can you see that they get back to my place this evening?"

"Sure," he replied. The three gave each other a casual, sexual once-over, evaluating, picking, choosing. Such an easy, unconfined sexuality these people have: if it moves, fuck it. If that wasn't entirely fair, I didn't care. Still, I moved, and nobody fucked me.

"Paul Ambuhl, Jenny Crane," I said, completing the introductions, and turned toward my car. Paul followed and laid a hand on my arm. I stared at the hand, shocked at the contact, waiting for him to withdraw it hastily and wipe it clean on the lining of his cape. But his hand stayed and I turned to face him.

"Tia, thanks for putting us up."

"No problem." I tried to move my arm, but he kept his light grip and, wetting his lips, continued.

"Look, have we done something wrong?"

"Wrong?"

"It's just that you're so, well, abrupt. I was wondering if maybe we'd, well, you know . . ."

"No, you haven't done anything wrong. Why don't you get back to Tobias now, okay? I've got an appointment in an hour."

I slipped away from him and into the driver's seat, starting the car before he had a chance to reply, and left him on the dock behind me, staring at the dust kicked up by the aircushions. I drove to the far end of the village, parked, and picked up a hopper for the short flight to the mainland. I wasted a few moments fuming over Paul's presumptive worries, then shrugged my anger away. One more evening and I would be free of them both. The *Ilium* sailed in the morning and I could easily avoid them once aboard. Flight, I thought wryly, heals all. I banished the bother from my mind.

9

By the time my arctic miseries had cleared and it was obvious that Paul was not following me from the hotel, I had evolved a plan which seemed, to my aching and melodramatic mind, in all ways perfect. My prior travels had been confined to the earth, following the unwritten dictum that children not yet old enough for the Immortality Treatments were to stay on the home planet. So the moon was a place Paul and I had not visited together, would hold no associations for me; he would not think of following me there, not after that final argument amid the gelid wastes. With all the drama of the young, pursued by my private furies, I determined to turn my back on the earth entirely, and two months after I left the clinic I boarded the shuttle to the city of Luna.

After the cushioned push of acceleration, the semi-gravity of the shuttle delighted me. I bounded through the cabin, touching the walls lightly, clumsy and soaring. Most of the other passengers remained seated or moved cautiously, clutching the handles affixed to the backs of the seats to make sure that they were at all times connected to something stable. I scorned their crablike uncertainties and bounced superciliously around them.

I made my way to the viewing cabin and moved through the dimness until my face was pressed against the port. The slight spin of the shuttle caused the universe beyond the safety of the walls to seem to revolve; the stars floated by in a stately, infinite dance. I tried to see the yellow glow of the space station, but it lay directly in front of the shuttle at that stage of the journey and could not be seen from the viewing port. I clung tightly to the rail, captured by the beauty of the stars seen through the clarity of vacuum until, part of the cosmic dance, the moon crept upward, astoundingly clear, pockmarked, beloved, beautiful.

"Impressive, eh?"

I turned reluctantly from the splendor of the moon and looked at the other occupant of the viewing cabin. He was a tall, broad man, with epicanthic eyes set above sculpted cheekbones, a large, hooked nose, and a thick beard covering his cheeks, chin, and upper lip. His hair, fairly closely cut, was still long enough to float about his head in the light pseudo-gravity as he nodded toward the rising moon. Massive, blunt fingers gripped the rail and one leg rested, bent, against the ribbed wall. The dim lights of the room washed all color from him, so that he seemed a mountain of blacks and greys and whites. I returned my attention to the port and nodded slightly.

"This is your first time to Luna and you're very young, right?"

"Yes," I replied, interested despite my desire to be left alone. "How did you know?"

"It's not hard to tell. The older you get, the less likely you are to be flying around the cabin, and since you're young enough to do that, and a little clumsy, you're young enough so that this is probably your first trip. About, what, twenty, twenty-one?"

"Does it matter how old I am?"

"No, not really. Just guessing. Nosy, eh? Are you going all the way to Luna?"

"Um."

"You might like it. Few people do, you know. Sure, they go up for the mining or the Library, the observatories, just to stare, but people don't usually *like* the place. You might, though. If you do, make sure you get out of Luna itself, get to some of the observatories, get up to the surface. It's not that dangerous."

"Have you gone out on the surface yourself?"

"Sure, it's part of my job. I work maintenance on the transport tubes, and about once a week we go out with crews and check things over, fix the places where small particles have broken through the tubes and been temporarily patched."

"I thought machines did that, robots and waldoes, not people."

"Machines make mistakes sometimes. And you can't trust a machine to make fast decisions the way a human can—the machines just can't pick up all the available data. Sure, you can trust them on Earth for work on some of the topside transport tubes, and other stuff, but on the moon the smallest mistake could cause a disaster. You have to watch out for things like that." He gave me a monochromatic grin across the plate of the port. "Tell you what, if you spend some time on Luna, give me a call. Name's Greg Hartfeld. The comsystem'll connect you with me. You want to get out on the surface, I'll take you along some time."

"Thanks," I said. "I'm Tia Hamley. I might spend quite a while up there. Maybe I'll give you a call."

"Good!" He smiled, kicked himself away from the wall with practiced grace, and soared out the door. I remained in the dimness, debating whether or not I wished to interrupt my self-imposed dramatic exile with the pleasantries of walks on the surface of the moon, or with the company of Greg Hartfeld. The moon, spectral and beautiful against the backdrop of the stars, moved out of sight beyond the lip of the port.

10

I landed the hopper in the unobtrusive lot in front of the hospital and climbed out. The building stood in a grove of pines, looking like nothing so much as a rustic nineteenth-century lodge—rough, wooden exterior, wooden balcony sweeping along the front of the building and around the right-hand corner, double-sashed windows, peaked roof, large stone fireplace—all of it fake, made of treated polymers, cushioned by force-fields. They'd done a good job of hiding the function of the building, but it still subtly announced itself as a hospital. They all do, for some reason, no matter how cunningly fashioned they are, no matter how much fear and terror lead to the disguise. Perhaps there is something in the air, something which announces "Here are maimed and tortured bodies, here are twisted spines and twisted souls, here lie the dying."

A floater lifted me over the fake wooden stairs and I entered the rusticized antisepsis of the waiting room. The receptionist ushered me to a bank and I sat patiently while my various prints were entered into the computer and confirmed. Then, as usual, I spent half an hour lying in the white-tinged forcebed waiting for them to begin. I gazed alternately out the window at the garden of blooming fuchsias and at the carefully colored walls of the ovoid room, so precisely designed to soothe angerephobic Immortals. How terrifying to be immortal, to have an eternity of youth to look forward to, and then to be ill, to be maimed, broken. How frightening to descend to the level of animals, for only animals sicken, only animals grow old, only animals die. Basic lesson of childhood, as important as the difference between little girls and little boys. How sad for the animals, for the cats and dogs and porcupines, who can't be Immortals, can't be eternally young, who must grow up and bear or engender young and grow old and die; that's it, the sum total of their existence, to have young ones and then pow! That's it. Thus the philosophizing of Tia at age seven, thus the ingrained and fought-against belief of Tia now, Tia who is one of those sad, sad animals.

So I lay in bed amid the oppressively pleasing colors and sympathized. I am resigned, I lied to myself, and basked in self-congratulations at my understanding of and compassion for those who needed the pastel tones.

All of which was wasted, of course. They floated me into the operating theater, and I felt the same ancient terror rising in my throat. My fingers ached to claw at the invisible, perfunctory straps, my legs tensed to run, and the shine of sweat covered my skin. I had an image to maintain, though, and smiled nonchalantly at the nurse as she applied the electrodes to my skull.

"Well, good morning, here we are again," she said jovially. She touched a lead and minute shafts of electronic anesthesia snapped through my brain. "How are we feeling this morning?"

She didn't expect an answer, and I couldn't give her the sarcastic one that waited behind my closed lips. I felt my muscles slacken, and the fog-fingers of drowsiness began to appear. I fought it as long as I could, while they floated me under the large machines, watched as they hooked the plastic veins in my right arm and neck to the transfuser. A surgeon busied herself with the sterile wrappings over my torso while someone sitting at a read-out board called out every minute, "All normal," or something to that effect—my hearing was becoming very fuzzy. I took my eyes from the surgeon and looked up at the curving bleachers, crowded with students, doctors, and other curious souls.

"All for me," I thought. "A whole fucking branch of medicine, all for me."

I must have said it aloud, for the nurse bent over my face, said, "Why, we're awake" and goosed her lead again. As she did so, I saw the doctor raise her hand in signal; the large machines hummed to life and I passed out gratefully.

I woke five hours later in my room. The windows were opaqued, the lights out, soft humming noises came from the machines connected to me. I lay still, feeling the last gobbets of slackness disintegrate, feeling the new blood rushing through my arteries. My chest ached from the marrow-tap, my belly from the pumping, but I soon felt my way beyond these small pains and into the real guts of me, into the complicated plumbing I hold inside. How clean everything felt—all the little machines, as they hummed and sloshed and thumped and gurgled in the middle of me. They'd cleaned out my lungs this time, and I felt the air moving through them, the oxygen absorbing into the soft pink lining and moving into my new blood, whispering its way up and down the channels and conduits; the tingling of cells in the layers of my skin; opening and closing of small petcocks, valves releasing minute flows into stomach and organs and bloodstream; smooth, rhythmic shuntings and pulsings; the tautness of muscle and ligament, the firmness of bone. I dove down, slipped through capillaries, floated through cavities of lungs and stomach, nestled briefly in the warmth of my womb, ignored, as usual, the unpleasant absence of my fallopian tubes, sensing, revelling in the feeling of freshness and life, convinced anew that I *would* live forever, with youth, health, eager energy. Then I opened my eyes and stared into the 'flector I had insisted they program into the ceiling. No change there. I confronted the same withered woman, lined and cracking, the same knowledge that all the shuntings and pumpings only served to move me closer to an inevitable death. Greying hair snaking around the face, lines around mouth and eyes, trailing tubes, electrodes, lines leading to the hulking machines beyond the walls. That's me, all right. I looked, fought bitterness, waited, and soon my insisted-on hour of post-operative privacy was ended, and the doctors and nurses and surgeons and technicians and orderlies and students and bed-pan cleaners trooped into the room, eager to begin their prodding and prying and examining and exclaiming. How they love me, these inquisitive troops! How they gloat over me, examine my least quiver and twitch, agonize over my urine and exult over my feces. They are all geriatric specialists, and I am their only possible patient; they follow me about the world, about the galaxy, waving their syringes and collecting bottles in the fond hope that I will allow them pieces of myself. And I do, of course: they keep me alive, they keep the rotting machines functioning as best they can. And pay me for the privilege, as had been promised decades ago, under a hot South African sun. I was generally pleased by the irony, that they provided me with enough money to do the dangerous things they so deplored. But I didn't let them in on the joke. After all, we are bound tightly together: no me, no them; no them, no me.

After a while they unhooked me from the monitors and trickled from the room, each one clutching a treasured piece of information—a bit of skin, a jar of urine, a small vial of sweat. I watched them make off with these minuscule parts of me and felt angry again. Dr. Hoskins chased the lingerers out, closed the door, and perched at the foot of my bed while I contained and disposed of the anger.

"Well, how are you feeling?"

I shrugged and sat back against the cool resiliency of the bed. I almost liked Hoskins. Generally, my doctors lasted between five and seven years before giving up gerontology, or, as was more likely (through, I hasten to add, no fault of my own), giving up medicine altogether. But Hoskins had trailed in my wake for almost eleven years, and I had grown, if not fond of her, then at least tolerant.

"As usual," I said, "thoroughly reamed out, all the pistons and gears functioning at peak again. How did it go?"

"Well. The kidneys won't need to be replaced for another year, but I want to keep an eye on the liver. The glands are working well. You shouldn't have any trouble there for, oh, another two, three years or so. We cleaned out the lungs."

"Yes, I noticed."

She moved her smooth round face into a quick frown. "I wish you'd tell us how you do that, moving into yourself that way."

Oh, how they all loved that question! I had heard it, with subtle and not subtle variations, over the past forty-five years, and had long since ceased to let it anger me. But the answer, like the mysterious pain in my back, was something I kept privately; let them poke and pry and postulate—these things, at least, were my own.

"I've told you," I lied. "It's all in the old books, the meditation, the inward-turning. It's simply a question of training."

"But you can't control it, can you?"

"I can control the awareness-state, sure. But I can't control what goes on inside me, any more than you can. I can only observe." And that much, at least, was true.

She tugged absently at her amber-colored hair, and the corners of her mouth tightened slightly in concentration. "You know that Dr. Evert spent ten years trying to do what you do." I nodded. "He simply couldn't get into it. He attained all the preliminary stages, but he just couldn't manage the last one."

"Perhaps," I suggested maliciously, "the Treatments make it impossible. Maybe you need to be dying to move inside yourself."

"Nonsense," she said curtly. She stood, shook a wrinkle from her sleek tunic, told me I could leave in another hour, and departed from the room, having asked her usual question and obtained the same answer. Time and again how it must have galled her to be faced with a problem she couldn't solve; a depth, corner, piece of me that she couldn't probe and analyze with her machines, her tapes, her knowledge. It pleased me that they could not plumb my psyche, that they could not suspect my pain. I rose from the bed, cleared the windows, and sat gazing at the flowering plants outside.

"Simply a question of training," I'd told her. As though I knew. For I'd been taken there by a short-cut, decades ago, while orbiting a furious sun. And knew little more of the process than she did.

11

Fifty years ago, I had left another clinic in a state of shock, tried to find solid ground beneath my feet, and failed.

It takes a while for big things to sink in, to find the proper level of consciousness, to take up full residence in the soul. I stumbled from the clinic into the hot South African sunlight and did not fully comprehend what had happened to me, what I had been told. Mortality was inconceivable and, as a child of the age, I did not have practice stretching the mind to the limits of understanding. On the cruiser headed north the great tides of it finally broke over me, and I sat shivering and alone, huddled in a corner of the ponderous airboat as it glided and bumped over veldt and savannah, over mountains and seas. When I stumbled out at Istanbul, I left behind not only the cruiser, but whatever childhood the world was to give me.

Istanbul is a quiet city. The restoration is complete, but very tiny; the mosque, some medieval palaces, a few cobbled streets, the bridge across the Bosphorus.

Fragrant plants grow along the tops of walls and the ledges of buildings, with great clusters of blossoms spilling down along the stones. Occasional soft music from distant, closed, cool rooms. Small cafes with one or two people sitting silently within them, waiting. A hot, bright sun.

City of dreams. City of silence. City of pounding sunlight. City with a thousand beds, and each one carrying an Immortal in stupor, head filled with gaudy images, scents and sounds, tastes and touches, body neatly tucked into its life-support station. A constant euphoria is purveyed in the city of dreams, an unchanging ecstasy, seductive, solemn, and silent.

I could, of course, have stayed at the port outside of town, at the great crossroads between the East and West, and never ventured into Istanbul. But I shouldered my bag and took the hopper into the city. What Immortal needed dreams more than I? To whom would constant fantasy be more useful? Oh, I was young, and stupid, and in shock, and grasped at the first escape that presented itself.

I could not go under immediately, for the couches were full, and had to wait two days until space could be made for me. I fled the cool peace of the hotel every morning, had coffee and cakes in a cafe, then wandered the city at length, peering at the newly-old buildings and streets, at the waters of the seas and the distant shoreline. I avoided the Immortals, half convinced that they could see my secret, that the vicious, invincible signs of aging already streaked across my face. I wore covering clingsuits through the heat, and kept my head well down, my body tense.

When the time came, I lay naked upon a brocaded couch and drank the sleeping potion from a crystal goblet. Once asleep, I knew, they would float me into the dreaming room, affix the tubes and wires of the life-support to me and, when all was set, would introduce the dreaming drug into my veins. I was more than ready.

Drug dreams come in strength and go quickly, and

I cannot remember what, exactly, they were, nor where, exactly, they took me. I do remember a world of wonder and light, an exotic garden of fantastical fruits and imaginary beings, an Eden I had created, and with which I could have my way. So easy, so easy, to spend the remainder of my life in this self-made paradise, letting my body slide gently into death while I wasn't around to notice. So very sweet.

But I couldn't do it. No matter what the ecstasy, nor how seductive the image, a small, rebellious thing in my brain told me that it was only a dream, not real, no substance. A fantasy. A fraud. And I could not vanquish the voice that pursued me through the mazes of my fantasies.

At the end of my forty-eight hours they unhooked the life-machines, brought me from the dream-state, and asked if I wanted to go in again. I said no and thanked them, slung my bag over my shoulder and left Istanbul, turned my back on dreams.

But not because I wanted to.

12

I backed my battered car down the landing groove into the garage and noticed a hopper parked by the door. Odd; who would be visiting here? Then I noticed the chrome, the dents on the back wings, the bright cerise seats. Tobias' hopper, but the driver's seat was pulled too far forward to accommodate that big bastard, and Tobias would never put his hopper under a roof. I was still puzzling it out as I walked slowly from the garage to the house.

Paul and Jenny sat on a lower balcony, one that twisted halfway around the side of a redwood cube, and they waved up at me as I approached the front door. Of course, they must have borrowed the hopper from Tobias and come up by themselves. Which meant, first, that my driving had terrified them more than I had thought and, second, that one of them must either have screwed with Tobias already or be planning to do so in the near future. Tobias never loaned anything without an assurance of getting some return for it. I waved back at them and entered the house,

clattered down the twisting wooden staircase, past the
bright stained-glass windows and the small ledges
covered with potted plants, and paused at the kitchen
level. My guests had already cooked themselves dinner; the counter by the sink was littered with emptied
food containers, and the preparations units displayed
unfamiliar settings. I tossed the garbage down the
chute and reset the controls on the units to my usual
specifications before continuing downward. At the foot
of the stairs I found two lift-packs, piled casually on
the bottom step. Lift-packs! Naturally, they would be
used to drop-shafts, but with their youth and health
they certainly should be able to cope with the stairs for
the one day remaining before we boarded the *Ilium*. I
was tempted to remove the power packs from the objects, but let them lie. My guests would garner quite a
few bruises trying to use them; the staircase did not
wind up the side of a central shaft, but coiled over
itself a number of times, creating its own ceiling. To
use the packs they would have to proceed very slowly
and with a fair amount of skill.

I had thought Paul and Jenny were naked, but as I
walked out onto the unprotected balcony I could see
the light shimmer of force-bubbles around them. Lift-
packs, hoppers—I told myself it would have been too
much to expect them to sit open to the air. Jenny gave
me a slight smile and waved her hand toward the sea.
"It's beautiful, isn't it? The sun behind us, and the
colors reflecting backwards. . . . I've never seen a
sunset on the sea from this angle."

I sat and gazed with them. "If you get up early tomorrow morning, you'll see the sunrise. The light appears over the far hills, there, then strikes the water.
It's spectacular."

Jenny nodded, her eyes still following the lingering
tracks of the backward sunset. I felt Paul's gaze on me
and turned to him. He looked at me with frank curiosity, nodded briefly and continued staring. Someone
on the *Ilium*, no doubt, had told them that I was off
having my valves reamed today, had described in

hushed tones their various misconceptions about my cleaning-out. I hoped that it had been Greville rather than Tobias; Greville would have explained his version in the solemn, prissy manner he had affected since becoming a "scientist," while Tobias would have spread his tales with all the fascinated terror of a child speaking of bogeymen. Well, it didn't matter, and I didn't expect Paul or Jenny to find me and my plumbing any less of a terrifying mystery than the others did. But Paul's look bothered me, the frank appraisal, things in his glance which I didn't want to see or cope with. I pulled my chair around so that he could see only part of my face.

"What do you think of the *Ilium?*" I asked.

Their comments were typical: beautiful, stunning, awesome, magnificent.

"And the possibilities," Jenny continued. "The forcefields, Benito explained them to me. He said that eventually they'll take the *Ilium* into space."

"Indeed they will," I replied. I wouldn't be around to see that, but I didn't think the comment would be appreciated. "Did Greville give you Lecture 1-A on the Meaning of It All?"

Jenny smiled. "Yes, we were thoroughly indoctrinated."

"You sink the entire ship, and just scoop up what's on the bottom," Paul said.

"It's more complicated than that, I'm afraid. Remember that the Islands sank during the Great Shaping, and aside from the damage from that, all sorts of things have accumulated down there. Water isn't the kindest preserving medium, and the silt and plants tend to hide a lot, too. Things aren't just lying about waiting to be picked up. They have to be probed for, looked for, uncovered. You have to know where to take time and what you might just as well leave be. And there are certain dangers under the sea."

"But Greville showed us the bubblesuits," Paul said. "They're as safe as being on the deck, he said."

"They are," I said sourly. "It's like taking a shell

along with you. Sure, you can see a lot, and you're protected, but you can't do anything or touch anything, and there's a lot of places you can't fit into. That's why they have remotes, to do your touching and doing for you."

"What's wrong with that?"

"First of all, seeing something yourself is much better than seeing something on a screen from a remote. And since remotes can get into places where bubblesuits can't, you're forced to rely on the screens, and the screens just aren't good enough, they can't concentrate on one given thing."

"But you can focus them, of course," Paul said, his hands making a small knob-turning motion in the air.

"Of course, and that's the second problem. It takes time for the image to come to you, and for you to send a command back to the remote. Granted, the time is short, but it's interminable compared to the time it takes an impulse to go from your fingers to your brain and back again. So the remote gives you a picture of, say, a vase. You command the remote to take it. But the vase turns out to be more fragile than it looks on the screen, and it's crushed. Take that incident and enlarge it, multiply it by ten for each dive, and you can see the problem."

"Tobias said you use a wet-suit," Jenny said. "Is that why?"

"And what's a wet-suit, anyway?" Paul asked.

"It's a skin-tight suit made of rubber," I said. "A pair of flippers for the feet, air tanks with hoses and regulators, a face-mask, weights to counteract the buoyancy of the rubber, small jets. I also have a radio keyed to the face-plate. And, yes, that's one of the reasons I use a wet-suit."

"And you go underwater just with that?" Paul asked. He shifted uncomfortably on the unfamiliar, solid chair and turned to face me more directly.

"Sure."

"But that's dangerous. You haven't any protection at all."

"Except a stunner. And my wits. Look, when you want certain results, you've got to evaluate the risks and take them. Or accept something second-rate, second-choice. Sure, scuba diving, wet-suiting, is more dangerous than floating around in your little completely protected forcefield, but if you want something you can't get using fields and remotes, you climb into a wet-suit and go down there yourself, and do it right the first time."

I hadn't realized how vehement I sounded until I glanced at them. They both wore the expression of pained attention people put on when they're forced to listen to nonsense from people they can't escape. I sighed, told myself that I should know better, and stood to go inside. The sun was completely gone, and the last strands of the sunset were darkening quickly into night.

"I've got to be up early. Remember that we have to be on board tomorrow by nine, okay?"

They assured me that they would be ready, bid me good-night, and I went in, still bothered.

⚔ 13 ⚔

In my mid-twenties I found myself completely alone for the first time in my life, tucked inside the research station that endlessly orbited the sun. Busy fleeing from the one place in the universe that I really wanted to be, from the one person I wanted to be with. In my grander moments I called it kismet, fate, the burden of mortality. In more common moments, I called it cowardice. Lexicographic distinctions, however, did not affect the station or my functions; I spun dizzily around Sol, measuring, metering, structuring time into neat blocks filled with neatly arranged activities. Each day my reports to Luna pulsed through, relayed from one booster to another along a wide curve from my station to the receiver at Johns-Rastegar, and half an hour later I would receive a reply from the base. No use hoping for a voice transmission this near the sun; the boosters had difficulty enough transmitting the varied bleeps and bonks of my signal without picking up an unacceptable amount of static. Had I anyone with whom I wanted to talk, I could tape my message and add it to the slim cargo I sent back each month in the supply shuttle, and wait another twenty-eight days until the shuttle, with message, came back to me. But there was no one I wanted to talk to, and the only voice I wanted to hear was, by now, approaching the orbit of Pluto.

I, or rather, the station's equipment, had tracked the course of that one place I wanted to be, as she circled the sun and, her velocity boosted, headed out through the solar system for the stars. Driven by curiosity and, perhaps, some subtle masochism, I had watched until the ship was beyond the range of my equipment, then slid into a depression that clouded my brain and left me pacing through my duties with no more thought or emotion than an android. When I finally pulled myself from the miasma, eight months later, the third anniversary of my arrival at the station was upon me, and I battled the remaining depression by structuring my secluded life along uncompromising lines. I set myself a goal and pursued it.

I studied Immortality. After all, I had long blocks of time to devote to no other activity, and I most certainly had the impetus for study. I requested an alternate-band transmission from Luna's Library, filled the station's extra tapes with everything the Library could send me on the subject, and set to work.

The Treatments work to create a state of nondegeneration, a state of physical stasis in the subject. They work on every primate above a certain evolutionary level. Certain chemicals affect the balance of certain glands, certain spirits affect the functions of certain processes, certain varieties of radiation control certain genetic commands. Or so they hypothesize. Bombard W areas with X amount of radiation for Y periods of time at Z intervals, and something shifts in the genetic structure, the degenerative processes cease. How does it happen? Why? No one exactly knows. Lippencott's papers abound with hypotheses and since-disproved theories, and the writings of his successors only serve to expand the areas of ignorance. The Immortals do not appreciate conundrums, and after the second century post-Shaping, research dwindled and, eventually ceased. It was enough that the Treatments worked, and seemed to work so successfully. I suspected that if the Immortals discovered an onset of deterioration at year thousand, research would re-open with unseemly haste. But year thousand, even for the oldest of the Immortals, was still far in the future, and I would not be around to benefit from any further inquiries.

I knew the basic structures of pre-Treatment human physiology, and the subtleties were available on tape. I knew the basic structures of post-Treatment physiology and, again, the subtleties were available. And I had my own tiniest specifications from before, during, and after the Treatments. I should have been able to pinpoint the reason for my lack of immortality. Hell, the scientists and doctors on Terra should have been able to do so, they had certainly pried and poked enough.

Yet the records showed no obvious anomaly in me, and people further from the mythic norm than I had been treated successfully. My post-Treatment records showed some slight changes that might or might not mean a tiny prolongation of my life beyond the pre-Shaping norm, but there was no definite explanation for what these small changes meant, or why they had appeared instead of the expected shifts to the immortality pattern.

The total of one year's constant study summed to this: the answer is that there is no answer, the reason is that there is no reason. I found this completely unacceptable. I needed more data, more knowledge, more tests. I needed more of myself, a further exploration. The small medical analyzers provided on the station were hopelessly unequal to the task, and I could not afford to import the delicate instruments my studies demanded.

For one month I battered at the stone walls of a dead end, and then I remembered Kai-Yu's drug.

More than scientific curiosity was involved in my

decision to trip again. Almost four years at sun station had left me desperately bored, despite the entertainments, the hobby rooms, the endless reams of tapes and cubes. And I was lonely. The only voice I heard other than my own, other than the canned voices of the tapes, was the stultified monotone of the computer, and its maddening sameness so infuriated me that I had programmed it to visual read-out only six months after boarding the station. The only sound of breathing was my own, mine the only footsteps, mine the only movements within the smooth egg of the station. I began talking to myself, expounding, singing, reciting, laughing. My daily transmissions became positively long-winded, and I awaited the responses to them eagerly. I taped wake-up signals for myself, and started each ship's day greeted by my own face and voice hovering over my bunk. And so, when I considered taking the drug, I decided that I was half out of my mind already, and going the rest of the way would not be too terrible.

And I had first taken the drug with Greg Hartfeld, during that brief, ecstatic, moon-bound time after Paul and before the station. I would never touch Greg again, for he and his friends had launched themselves and their ship out beyond the system, and I had watched them leave. In a convoluted way, the drug was one last link with him. That was important.

If one can hallucinate an outer world, one can hallucinate an inner world. Or so I told myself. I fasted for one day, just to make sure that the drug reached my system without picking up anything from the synthetic food on which I lived. The next morning, I quickly swallowed three drops of the drug with a cup of water, before I could change my mind, before I could remember the nightmares of my previous dream-voyage. I centered my mind on myself, lay back, and waited for the drug to take effect.

I concentrated on my lungs, on the moving of air through my throat, the expansion and decline of my chest. It was surprisingly easy to monitor myself this way, to pare my attention down to one particular part of me, and I filled my mind with the sensations of breathing. So deep was my concentration that I did not notice the point at which I slipped into the drug-state, the point at which I made the transition from feeling my lungs to being in them. At the time it seemed entirely normal.

I watched the complexity of my lungs at work, then pushed and prodded my way through them into my blood vessels, and using them as the highways of my progress I explored heart, digestive tract, various organs, sneaked into my capillaries and thence to the cells. Tapped into the spinal column and worked my way to the brain, tasting, poking, watching, feeling. When I felt the drug-state slip from me, I rose and took another three drops, and three hours later took some more, and more after that, until twenty hours had passed. The computer was gibbering frantically, the read-out screens pulsed helter-skelter up and down the spectrum and the vial was dry.

Johns-Rastegar was incoherent with worry. I had missed one full transmission, something unprecedented, and coils of material waited to be bleeped and bonked and buzzed down the transmission channels to the receiver. I assured the base of my continued health, programmed and pulsed the information down the line, and generally set things to rights before taking time to assess the information I had gained from my inner explorations.

Nothing new, nothing not already on my tapes, with one exception. I still had no idea why the decaying lump of matter that traveled with me insisted on aging, had no added knowledge of the reason for my impending death. My personal agglomeration of fat and tissue and suet and bone was as much a mystery now as it had been before the trip, and I considered it sourly, bitterly, and with hatred.

Then my stomach began complaining of emptiness and I found myself actually watching it, feeling each

insistent contraction, monitoring the drippings and secretions accumulating within it.

Marvelous, I thought as I punched random buttons
on the food unit. Great. Not only does the damned
thing have to fall apart, I get a ringside seat to watch it.
Fantastic.

It wasn't until much later, when the damned thing
really did start falling apart, that I appreciated what
the gift of monitoring meant; I could forestall various
complications by discovering them in their early stages,
and head them off by requesting appropriate treatment. Yet I found it but a minor consolation in the face
of death.

14

The pain caught up with me that night as I emerged from the vibra; it grabbed me along my back with such force that I gasped and held to the side of the door. I'd been warned—the episode on the roof balcony last night, the small twinges I'd ignored throughout the evening. I should have paid attention, but there was no help for it now. I fell to my knees, refusing to cry out, and waited for the first great wave to pass. It seemed an age, and when it had finished with me I staggered to my feet, bathed in sweat, and fell over the bed. I lay face down across the firm water-mattress and held tightly to the sides while the next, greater wave built at the base of my spine and pushed through me, twisting my back, grabbing the muscles and ligaments of my abdomen and wrenching them out of shape. The pain engendered a curious duality as part of me lay on the bed, twisting, and part of me followed with almost clinical detachment the tightening of muscles, the sudden contractions of the uterus, the gathering tautness of ligaments, the knots and bunchings which created and followed pain. The part of me twisting, the pain-part, demanded surcease, demanded that something be done, but I was helpless to control my body, could only observe, unable to find a way inside the pain to stop it. The second wave subsided; I lay shaking; my fingers ached from their grip on the wooden rails of the bed. The beginning, I thought before the next spasm. The metamorphosis into the grasshopper. Then I drowned once more.

When it passed I found Paul sitting on the bed, his hands on my quivering shoulders.

"Tia? Tia? Are you all right?"

"No."

"Shall I call a doctor?"

"No! No, they'll just . . . no, they won't help."

"Are you sure?"

"Paul, for God's sake, don't call a doctor!" The next wave came toward me. "Please, just believe me, don't call anyone, please, . . ."

"Can I help at least?"

"Yes. Put your palm on the small of my back and push!" I stopped talking, just concentrated on surviving the pain. I could feel Paul's hands on my back, pushing hard, and the pain lessened but not by much. That wave left me in tears, my anger and bitterness completely forgotten. Paul stroked my back, whispering.

"Tia, please, don't cry, please, let me call a doctor, please don't cry, Tia, please."

"Just push when it comes back," I said. Speaking was an effort. I had to draw long ragged bursts of air into my lungs before I could continue. "It'll be over, I'll, soon, just push now, now, NOW!"

He pushed. He pushed for two hours, until the pain had finished playing with my body and receded, leaving, as always, a promise to return. I lay quietly, putting myself back together while Paul brushed the twisted hair from my face with gentle fingers.

"Is it over now?" he asked as I opened my eyes.

"For this time. Yes." I rolled over, not bothering to worry about his reaction to my body, and lay limp, draining away the remaining tension. Paul, too, was covered with sweat and shaking slightly.

"Were you in great pain?"

"Yes."

"Why don't you let a doctor . . ."

"Paul, they go over me with microscopes every two months. They peer and pry in every fold and corner of me. There's nothing wrong that they can find."

"Do they know about the pain?"

"No," I said and didn't elaborate. It's all psychosomatic, anyway, part of being the sad animal. "It's just me turning into a grasshopper," I muttered. "It can't be helped."

"A grasshopper?"

"Forget it, nothing." I swung my legs over the edge of the bed and sat. "Why are you in my room, anyway?"

"I heard you. I was getting ready for bed and heard you, and when I called at your door you didn't answer, so I came in."

"Oh. I didn't think I was that loud." I paused. "Where's Jenny?"

"With Tobias, at the dock."

I nodded, remembering the borrowed hopper. I stood carefully, walked to the bathroom, and closed the door behind me. When I returned to the bedroom, showered and damp, I expected Paul to be gone. He sat on the bed, watching me, so I stood and let him get his fill, waiting for him to make some brittle excuse and flee. He didn't move, just watched me. Then he rose, walked to me, and kissed my mouth, so stunning me that I didn't react. He moved his head back and dropped his hands to my shoulders, then let his palms follow my body until they cupped my breasts.

"Remember Venice?" he said softly.

I nodded. Indeed, I remembered Venice, although I'd never been back since that one trip with him, before the deluge. His mouth came down again to cover mine, and he slid his hands to my back and pressed me closer. Then, carefully, he carried me to the bed, pulled the covers around my shoulders, slipped in beside me, and cradled me in his arms. Half convinced that I was dreaming, I fell asleep.

And he was still there in the morning when the sunlight coming through the stained glass of the eastern windows woke me. I turned over and felt his arm, his back, opened my eyes and stared, remembering the evening before. He woke, rolled over, smiled at me and placed a hand on my breast.

"Do you know what you're doing?" I asked.

He smiled an assurance and continued caressing me, until I felt stirrings that I'd believed to be long dead, buried under the layers of my desiccation. Amazed, I touched his body, felt his erection, the smooth sweep of his back, the tense eagerness of his buttocks as he lifted himself and entered me. The remaining weakness and the eons since I'd last screwed made me ungainly, unable to match his pace, but he moved for both of us and my body surprised me by coming, the ecstasy moving through the places that had so lately been filled with pain and making them whole again. Paul, careful lover, took his time, moving slowly, slipping my name into my ear before his tongue, and when he came I held him and rocked us on the bed. The intensity of his orgasm and his cries tipped me over the verge into ecstasy again. Suspicious even in joy, I wondered at the why of it, whether he'd needed someone to screw and in his need accepted even me, whether he'd made a bet with someone, Jenny, perhaps. But he held himself above me and gave me a smile of such radiant pleasure that my suspicions fled and I smiled back. After a while we made love again, this time with the blankets kicked to the floor, naked bodies twined on the bed. And, coming again, I felt forever youthful, for the first time in fifty years.

15

Fifty years ago I owned Venice. Or thought I did. The Great Shaping had taken even the soggy remains of the city and eaten them, but the city had been reconstructed under the now pure waters of the Adriatic Sea. Clear water shimmered over the ancient city; reconstructed palaces gleamed from their protective force-bubbles; fish scurried through the plazas, skimming by crystal windows, and darted through the columns and walls of the rebuilt ruins. Bubble-encased visitors moved dreamlike, trailing light. Venice. Stepping from the transport tubes, Paul and I slipped under the skin of the water, deep into the gold and blue and scarlet, into mazes of stone and softness, into brocades, marble, velvet, granite, silk. The child that was me breathed deep, convinced that the air was of a different time, the lingering perfumes and incenses of ages past. I held Paul's hand and skipped through the corridors round-eyed with awe, sent clear laughter sparkling through the clear, pure city. The guidetapes said Venice had been a dirty city, but I didn't believe it. We danced with fish in the sunlight, ate and drank in rooms that still echoed the music of other voices and other times. I bought a plum-colored cloak and a white ruff, and Paul bought a plumed hat; together we stalked through reconstructed halls, playing at doges and ladies until we spun into each other's arms, gasping, and sought quiet corners for our lovemaking. We found a room of mirrors, and I still see clearly a child with billows of auburn hair and a rounded, bronzed body, dressed only in spreading cloak and ruff, dancing lightly over her own reflection with the slim beauty that was, that is, Paul. I think we were both in love, in Venice, with Venice, with ourselves, with each other.

From Venice I went back to South Africa, and all the mirrors changed.

Now, ages later, lying with Paul in an archaic bed overlooking the Pacific Ocean, I fought again the battle with bitterness. This is Paul, I told myself, the same Paul who danced with me in rooms of crystal, who ran with me through arching flights of stone. Who remembers the forgotten child, the Tia who was? Who loved that child? Yes, certainly, but did he love, could he love what that child had become? I remembered the intensity of his excitement as he entered me and wondered if he was screwing Tia then or Tia now, and if Tia now, then why? One question led to another, and another, and I refused them life, banished them to the dungeons of my mind, barred the gates against them. Do not poison, do not deny, accept, I instructed myself. And I accepted.

❧ 16 ❧

"Hullo, lover. Slumming, are we?"

I turned quickly against the hot Australian desert wind, peering through the sunlight at the figure that had materialized behind me. The voice was not at all friendly.

"No. Not exactly."

The voice made a skeptical noise. Whoever it was stood against the falling sun, and I could barely make out a figure. The figure seemed to stare at me, and I cringed involuntarily, bringing my hands up to grab my shoulders.

"One of us, then," the voice said positively, and laughed. "Marvelous, lover, just great. Come along, then, no use your standing there getting baked." The figure moved, grabbed my bag, and paced off toward the terminal. After a moment's hesitation I followed, trying to rub grit from my eyes.

Australia, land of bogey-men, shadows, rumor, and fear; the home of nightmares and rejects. Immortals whispered about its horrors, and children used the

name to frighten each other. I had expected to be met
by a welcoming party of walking nightmares, a delega-
tion of horrors, and I squinted, but could not make out
the details of my companion against the fiercely setting
sun.

My bag was raised to eye level, turned about for
a thorough inspection, lowered again.

"From Istanbul? Well, you've done the route, then.
Know what we call this place? Damnation Springs,
Australia. There's a frog's lot of us here, lover, but
you'll meet us all. You got a queasy stomach?"

"I don't think so."

"Good." We stepped into the cool shadows of the
terminal and my companion turned, smiling. A missing
arm, a violent birthmark across the face and down the
neck, one solid eyebrow running from temple to temple, a dark light within the eyes. And, beneath the
ugliness, a face of almost breath-taking regularity, the
lineaments of beauty. The smile was real.

Her name was Sal. She left her face that way because if she didn't have yearly surgery on it, it re-
verted, so why bother? She'd lost her arm in a hopper
accident. She'd been a tourist guide in London before
then, and knew it and its history with such comprehension that I sometimes accused her of making it up.
She'd taken on the job of greeting new ones arriving
at the Springs, and of chasing away those strange Immortals who thought of the population as a tame
circus. She took me under her wing, into her house,
into her bed. Showed me around, introduced me.
Didn't ask what my particular freakery was.

And I learned quickly that no one asked at Damnation Springs. It was enough that you were there; you
were immediately included in the roster of the world's
rejects and were left to the privacy of your own particular difference. Some, like Sal, were obvious: missing
arms or legs, physical damages so bad that nothing
could disguise them. Medicine under the Immortals
was advanced, yes; but there remained things they
were unable, or unwilling, or afraid, to cure. Others

bore their changes internally, and since I was not obviously physically damaged, I was taken to be one of the crazy ones. It suited well enough.

Patterns within patterns in the arid desert. A cell of people intent upon the overthrow of the Immortal way of life; the others called them the Freakery Forever sect, and they grew ever more impotent and angry under the jibes. They spent their time painting slogans on sheets of paper, which they plastered to all available surfaces in the dingy village. The paper shredded and dried almost immediately, and the buildings were covered with beards of illegible slogans. I asked Sal how long they'd been active, and she shrugged. Just outside of town was a commune governed by a fanatic who spent his time railing at and against his apathetic followers. He read them hunks from self-made religious books, creating a total confusion of thought to which they listened absently, sitting in the dust picking at scabs or each other. Sal and some others brought them food from town, dragged them to the hospital when they needed it, buried those who died. The fanatic never seemed to notice.

The hospital was the hardest place to take, and after the first visit with Sal, I refused to go back. It seemed not so much a place of healing as a place of waiting, crammed with wounds and dullness. The doctors were all on assignment from Berne: Damnation Springs, for a doctor, was a punishment detail, and they made no effort to hide their disgust. One of them, taking me aside, offered me a bottle of beer to go to bed with him. Sal broke his arm, and the next day he left, still screaming. I think he thought she was contagious.

The children's ward was the worst. Sal and I had picked up four new ones that day: a man confined within a confusion of waldoes, a woman with the withdrawn look of madness about the corners of her lips, and two children. We took the waldoed man to a hostel and the madwoman to the commune, where she immediately sank into the thick apathy. I sat in the battered hopper with the children in my arms. The boy fell asleep against my shoulder; the girl, less trusting, finally put her lips against my neck and slept. I tried not to shudder: they had thick pink scars running down their faces, puckered and ugly. The girl's right eye had disappeared into the scar-tissue; the boy's hands were permanently clenched. They could, neither of them, have been above seven years old.

"Fire," Sal said prosaically, as she guided the hopper toward the hospital. "Probably too extensive for an adequate clean-up."

"But, if just a little work was done, enough for the hands, or another eye—"

Sal shrugged. "They're alive. That's all the parents are required to do, take steps to keep them alive. They probably didn't want to look at the results, even after clean-up." She glanced at the sleeping children. "Can't blame them."

"They sent them here," I said, feeling cold despite the hard light. Sal didn't bother to answer. As we pulled up before the dark hospital, I held the children tightly.

"Let's take them home," I said. "I'll care for them, we can expand the stipend. I'll pay for them. Someone ought to want them, even if it's only us."

But Sal shook her head and carefully pried the children from my arms.

"They die," she said. "Here, at least, they die in company."

When I saw the children's ward, I understood what she meant. There was room for sleep and room for play, classrooms and gardens and yards, toys and books, plentiful food. Enough to keep them alive, enough to keep them interested and educated. The children used none of it. Why should they? They were the children of Immortals, they had been taught the same lessons I'd learned as a child. And they'd been sent to bogey-land, had been consigned to hell.

They killed each other.

I couldn't have children—they'd done that for me in South Africa. To maintain the purity, they'd explained to me. After all, did I want to put a child into the same position I was in?

For the first and only time I was glad of that. I never went back to the children's ward again.

I followed Sal everywhere, peering, prying, trying to discover another one like me or, barring that, a situation among the freaks where I could spend my life. No libraries. No laboratories. No schools, aside from the unused rooms in the children's ward. A graveyard, yes—but there were no deaths here from natural causes. They killed themselves or, more rarely, each other. They died of their diseases or disfigurements, not of age. They were freaks, but Immortal freaks, and their sense of oneness was also a prejudice against change, against chance, against reaching out. Their rejection by the mainstream of the culture made no difference in their view of the world. Freaks, yes, but they were not animals.

I, of course, was.

Gentle, violent Sal held me in her arm, pressed my face against her breast as I wept. Assumed that I was simply getting used to the life, to the people, to my own eternity of difference. I would adjust, she assured me, her fingers wrapped gently in my thick hair. It would be all right. I clung to her until the shaking stopped and I could speak to tell her that I had to leave.

She didn't believe me, and when I finally convinced her she stood and left my bed, paused at the door, and glared at me.

"You'll be back," she said coldly. "Coward."

Coward, I thought, and caught the shuttle to Melbourne, to Beijing, to Diablo, to the Pole, to the moon.

17

We were closing the house when Jenny arrived. Paul stood on the balcony, handing the shutter-bars up to me as I balanced on the edges of the large windows, carefully placing the bars across the protective shutters. He had looked at the thirty-foot drop from the window to the rocks below and refrained from offering further assistance. Toting the bars after me, he asked if it wouldn't be simpler to install repellors around the house. Of course it would be simpler, but it would not be fitting, not right. He wanted to know why not. I tried to explain to him, tried to explain about the redwood and stained glass, about the solid furniture and the alien kitchen, about the rightness of things being what they were meant to be. He didn't understand, and eventually I gave up trying. So he stood patiently handing me the bars and I fastened them in place, contemplating the distance between us even as his hand rested on my thigh for a moment before moving to grasp another bar.

Jenny arrived in the hopper, parked it, and lifted easily over the edge of the cliff. The day was warm, the breeze cool, and she was, for once, dressed. The soft, slitted tunic changed color in the wind and floated about her body, baring her hips as she descended. I twitched the collar of my usual opaque jumpsuit, then caught myself, grimaced, and continued latching the shutter.

"Hello," she called, and alighted gently as a leaf on the balcony. "Do you want to use my lift-pack?"

"No, thanks," I said. "I'm almost finished anyway."

From the corner of my eye I saw her glance at Paul, who shrugged in reply, amused, and handed me the last bar. I finished my work and climbed down to the balcony to join them.

"Did you see the sunrise this morning?" I asked Jenny.

She remembered our conversation of the night before and gestured lightly. "I was busy," she said, and grinned. Paul grinned back. "So were we," he said.

"Oh? Closing the house that early?"

"Not quite." Paul gathered the bindings of the shutter-bars together. "Tia, where do I put these?"

"Under the stairs, to the right as you enter. The door's open," I said. He shouldered his way into the house, arms full.

"Are you all packed?" I asked Jenny.

She avoided my eyes. "Yes, I've just got to take the stuff down. I brought the hopper, I thought it might be easier that way."

"Well, we have to be at the dock in about an hour, so maybe you'd better start taking your stuff to the hopper." She nodded and went inside. I heard her speaking with Paul, then the smooth whisper of the lift-pack as she elevated up the stairs, and a second smoothness as Paul followed.

My things, with the exception of some personal items which I kept with me, were already aboard the *Ilium*. After I turned off the kitchen equipment and set the plants' caretaker on automatic, I climbed the stairs to my bedroom. It would only take me a minute to pack. The voices of my guests floated down to me as I paused on the landing by my door.

"Paul, aren't you packed yet?"

"No, but it'll only take a minute."

"I thought you were going to pack last night," she said. I could hear the sound of clothes being floated from the closet toward the bed.

"I didn't have time to."

"Oh? Stargazing all night?"

"Not exactly."

"Good lord, what else is there to do around here? It's a wonder Tia doesn't die of boredom, with nothing to do but watch the tide come in. Well?"

"Well, what?" A stubborn tone, an echo of fifty years back.

"What did you find so exciting to do last night?"

"I fucked with Tia."

A long pause. It wasn't the word I'd have used, I told myself blankly, and could not move.

"You . . . with Tia?" Jenny said finally.

"Sure. You were busy with Tobias. . . ."

"You bedded that—that *freak*—"

"Perish, Jenny, be reasonable—"

"Reasonable! She's not even human! You're—you're unsynched, Paul. You need help." Her voice shook.

"Jenny—"

"Don't touch me!" Jenny screamed, and I ran into my room, slapped the lock, and stood clenching my fists and my teeth. No human? Me? Tia? Twinges in my spine, wrinkles on my face, trapped in the workings of time—hell, I was more human than any of them. I was in direct descent from the apes, from Donne and Heisenberg, from Petrukis and Penderevcki, from Li Po and Lippencott, the Father of Immortality, who discovered the treatments too late to save himself. And they? Lippencott's Children? Super-

men, perhaps, but not human. No, of course not, absolutely, definitely not human.

And how I envied that inhumanity.

Silence from above. I opened the window, breathed the salt air deeply, calmed myself, and began packing. I heard Paul lifting luggage from the upper bedroom balcony to the hopper, and soon Jenny joined him. They worked in silence, and when I thought they were finished I slung my bag over my shoulder and clattered upstairs.

Jenny had already left, the hopper gliding quickly down the road, secure in its webs of force. I stowed my bag in the back of my car.

"I guess I'll be going down with you," Paul said, smiling. His face was easy, body tense.

"Okay. Does Jenny have your stuff?"

"Yes." He climbed into the passenger seat, pulled the safety webbing firmly about him and gripped the seat, prepared to defy death. I slid into my seat, webbed in and started the rotors. I considered briefly whether I should mention their overheard conversation, decided against it, put the car in gear, and shot out of the garage. Paul maintained his white-lipped quiet and his desperate grip on the seat all the way to the dock.

❧ 18 ❧

One week after I'd arrived at Luna I decided that I
wanted to stay, and found an apartment near the
Library. The apartment was small; I wasn't used to
the cramped quality of life on the moon, just as I
wasn't used to the gravity, and spent my first week in
the apartment banging into things at every turn. The
landlady, downstairs, laughed, called my bruises
"earthbadges" and provided salves. I soon picked up
the knack of moving without constant disaster, the
habit of sliding downstairs by the central shaft and
bending my knees just so as I touched bottom, of lop-
ing rather than walking and soaring rather than running. I liked the freedom of it, liked the freshness
programmed into the air of Luna, liked the sense of
living protected amid the wastes. The day a tourist
asked directions of me, I was elated.

I explored the city, moving first through the vaulted
passageways on the lower levels near my apartment.
How odd to see a blue sky overhead, and know that
I was fifty meters underground, and know that the

same blue sky shone down on the level above my own. Carefully created vistas greeted me in unexpected places: I turned a corner on my way to the galleries and found an open meadow on my left, so real in appearance that I had to walk into the projection to convince myself that it was only a holo. "Home-like," my Luna-born landlady told me, yet Earth had never been her home. Wandering under the programmed stars one night, I found an anomaly in the dense city: an acre or so of dwellings completely uninhabited, illuminated by dim, diffused glows emanating from the walls. The walls were hacked from lunar rock—undisguised, naked, raw. No veneers here, just the stark simplicity of stone, although the empty apartments each boasted force-furniture and -walls, complete kitchen units, self-programming holo-sculptures, everything. I asked my encyclopedic landlady about it the next day and she was surprised by my surprise. "Not home-like," she said, "uncomfortable." She told me, though, of a complex at Gagarin that looked exactly like Luna's empty apartments, although Gagarin's stone houses were carefully constructed of plasteel and 'crete, and were immensely popular. I remembered Greg Hartfeld's comment in the shuttle concerning the dislike of tourists for the moon itself, and expanded his statement to include those born or living on the moon. I spent much time in the viewing chambers, staring rapt at the stark frigidity of the moon's surface, and more often than not I was alone there. The Immortals did not care for the sight of the close-horizoned emptiness outside their secure dome. I discovered more and more that there was no essential difference between the Earth I had fled and the Luna I had chosen; the difference, perhaps, between a garden and an exact copy of that garden in miniature. The inhabitants of the gardens were identical—comfortable stasis, fear of the new or different, and a view of the future as one broad, clean repetition of today and yesterday.

Even my landlady had been a sand-jockey on Mars twenty years earlier, and told endless stories of thick-domed hydroponics gardens pallid under an equally pallid sun, of ferrying supplies by surface barge over the dry red dunes, and the boisterous life in the cantinas and whorehouses of Yurigrad—cantinas and whorehouses carefully designed to look, of course, like those on Earth. When I asked her to tell me about Mars itself, about the wastes, about the dunes, the tracks, the way the stars looked, she shrugged and said she'd never noticed, and changed the subject. She insinuated that Luna, too, began to bore her, and talked about an endless series of possible future professions: medicine, perhaps, or the law, or some form of the arts. She knew almost nothing about any of these subjects, but there was no hurry, she had eternity in which to learn, practice, discard, choose again. All the time in the world, and nothing would change between now and then. The consciousness of my own hidden difference rose to pursue me again; by the time my landlady had decided on and entered another field, I would probably be dead. I avoided the company of the Immortals and spent more and more time in the labyrinthine wonders of the Library of the Moon.

Luna is a dense city, crammed, with not an inch of wasted space. Yet the Library sat on a carefully tended square acre of grass; a huge, breathtaking sculpture. Only the first two levels of the building were visible from the surface; constructed in articulated deltoids, cantilevered one over the other and constantly bathed in washes of textured light, they seemed both immense and airy, both rooted and poised on the brink of flight. These first levels contained rooms, vaults, chambers, echoing halls crammed with materials, and these were only the indexes. The main bulk of the building, bursting with copies and occasional originals of everything Earth and her colonies had produced, corkscrewed deep into the lunar rock. Each level lay like a cross-section of a citrus around the main well, with corridors and more rooms moving tangentially from the center, honey-combing under the city. The Library sank deeper into the moon than the city itself, but those sections of the Library that were level with the city had their own openings, and were dedicated to different subjects, so that a scholar could take up residence on, say, section three of Luna, study and research physics on level three of the Library, and never have need to move vertically through either city or Library. For those who did wish to move among levels and subjects, the Library provided lift-packs, and the central core served as a great highway through the building. From the top deltoid of the Library, I looked down the central well and saw the lights of the levels extending below me until they were small, bright dots in the distance, and I still wasn't sure that I'd actually seen the bottom of the building.

I spent the bulk of two months in the Library, moving through large, echoing rooms rarely occupied by anyone other than myself, flitting on my lift-pack from level to level as I read through eons of thought about mortality, about aging, about death. Read scientists and mystics and religious doctrine and poetry; viewed tapes of people dying; contemplated sculpture and paintings, found Petrukis' *Andromeda Mourning* and stood paralyzed before it for ninety minutes; listened to dirges and requiems until my head reeled.

"The best way not to die too soon is to cultivate the duties of life and the scorn of death," I was advised in one tome, yet the Immortals about me lived in fear of death and maiming, and would live forever. "Never send to know for whom the bell tolls," an English mystic called to me. But the bell would toll for me only; there were no other inevitable candidates. And would my death diminish anyone at all? "When we exist there is no death, and when there is death we do not exist," Epicurus pontificated; how was I to draw com-

fort from that spare philosophy? "Do not go gentle
into that good night. Rage, rage against the dying of
the light." Ah, how I envied the Ancients, for when
they cried of death and aging, their cry was a universal one, and not the unintelligible howl of one starving
in the midst of feast. Yet, "neither his class nor his
kind nor his trade may come near him,/There where
he lies on his left arm and will die." Very well, very
well. The Ancients also died alone. It didn't help. I
listened to a threnody composed for the victims of
man's first atomic stupidity and found passion and
anger and fear, but no comfort, nothing to guide me.
What did any of it matter? People had died, until
comparatively recent times people had always died,
there were no exceptions, no one escaped. People had
invented various philosophies to explain or comfort,
but they still died and were blown to nothingness,
and there wasn't anything they could do about it. I
read through films of novels and stories containing the
guesses of my ancestors about immortality, and
laughed in the empty rooms at the worlds of wonder
they so eagerly created.

These explanations held no place for me. When I
died I would die, too soon, too early, alone, and become a case history in some convoluted medical text,
filed in an as-yet-undiscovered room of this same
building. No wings of angels or demons of hell, no
Valhalla, Elysian Fields or River Styx. I observed the
tapes, read the books, and stared at sculpture and
paintings until I imagined death stalking me behind
every soft whisper of filtered air, behind every distant
footfall in the vaults of the Library. Erinyes? For what
crime I was pursued? Did I hear banshees wailing in
the distant stacks? That sudden, ominous rumbling,
was it some simple machine or something darker,
deeper, something coming to rid the world of its one
true freak? Tia Hamley had brought mortality into a
world of youth, should she not then be suitably punished by the Gods?

I fled the Library, returned all the films and tapes
I had borrowed, destroyed my notes, erased my
tapes, and kept the one piece that spoke to me of all
I had studied. An elegy written by a young man in
the Tower of London, in Britain, the evening before
he was executed for some crime that history has
not bothered to record:

> My prime of youth is but a frost of cares,
>> My feast of joy is but a dish of pain,
> My crop of corn is but a field of tares,
>> And all my good is but vain hope of gain;
>>> The day is past, and yet I saw no sun,
>>> And now I live, and now my life is done.

Chidiock Tichborne, what were you thinking as you
died? Was the sun shining? Or was the city smothered
in fog? Was it spring? Autumn? Summer? Winter?
Were many people there, or only you and the execu-
tioner, and such notables as were necessary to make
sure you were dead? Did you cry out in protest or remain silent? Did you accept the comforts of your religion or did you have one? Did you joke?

> My tale was heard and yet it was not told,
>> My fruit is fallen and yet my leaves are green,
> My youth is spent and yet I am not old,
>> I saw the world, and yet I was not seen;
>>> My thread is cut and yet it is not spun,
>>> And now I live, and now my life is done.

Did you love someone? Did someone love you? Did
you know your parents, and did they grieve? Did
friends lift sad toasts to you? Did anyone rejoice in
your death? Did your death make any difference, or
none at all? What did you do with your hands? And
your feet? Did you look at the sky or at the trees? Did
you foul your clothes in fear, or did you feel any fear
at all? What were your last words? Did you cry?

> I sought my death and found it in my womb,
>> I looked for life and saw it was a shade,
> I trod the earth and knew it was my tomb,
>> And now I die, and now I was but made;

My glass is full, and now my glass is run,
And now I live, and now my life is done.
Chidiock Tichborne, if I die in fifty years or a hundred, I will be as young to my world as you were to yours. You cannot comfort me, but you make me feel less alone.

19

Jenny had taken the hopper directly to the *Ilium*, leaving the deck hopper for Paul and me. I keyed open one of the storage garages and parked my car inside, and we took the hopper to the ship, landing on the mosaic flight-deck beside the largest of the minarets. Tobias' hopper was parked off to one side, still loaded with luggage. Jenny was gone. Paul shrugged, took his own luggage from Tobias' cerise machine, and started toward the lift-tube.

"Where's your cabin?" he said as I followed him.

"Third level. Why?"

"Well, it looks like Jenny's not going to want me in hers. . . ."

"Why not?" I stepped into the tube and clenched my teeth against the quick, stomach-lurching descent.

"We had an argument about Tobias," he said blandly, as we dropped.

Dishonest bastard, I thought angrily. "Well, if you

and Jenny are assigned together, that's where you'll be. Unless you want to make other arrangements with Greville. I'm sure he'll find you something suitable." I stepped off at the third level. "I'll see you in half an hour on the bridge. Usual presailing pep talk from Greville. We're not supposed to miss it."

Paul, looking unhappy, dropped out of sight. I walked quickly to my cabin, still angry at the lie.

My cabin sat sterile and empty, waiting for me to bring it to life, to key in the forcefields and create beds, tables, chairs. Instead I turned off all the fields, then slung my hammock from the two hooks I'd previously affixed to the walls. I uncovered my bookshelves, brought my desk from the storage area and assembled it, and set up the folding chair. One bright orange blanket tossed on the hammock, one rug on the floor, and I considered my cabin fit to live in again. I showered quickly, climbed into a light clingsuit, knotted my hair behind my head, and, half an hour up, made my way to the bridge.

Greville and Harkness were conferring by the large holomap of the Northern Pacific. Jenny, huddled beside Tobias, peered mournfully out of one of the large windows; they turned to look at me as I entered, then Jenny faced the window again. Paul slouched against the wall opposite them. He started toward me, but I turned my back on him and greeted Benito, the hunch-backed Chief Engineer.

"Hello, ugly," I said.

"Hello, ugly," he replied, and scowled. I sat beside him and we shared a companionable, contemptuous silence. I could see Paul lean back against his wall, with a strange expression on his face. He'd met Benito, of course, the previous day, but the engineer was always something of a shock, even to those Immortals who worked around him. That he was not in Australia was, to me, a source of wonder and awe; I could never, I thought, begin to match his courage. But I was not about to tell him that.

Li came in, late as usual, slid into a field-chair to

my right, and wriggled to adjust the field to his ample
bulk. Jenny and Tobias moved from the window and
sat near Hart and Lonnie. Paul, finally, accepted a
seat at Lonnie's side. We were assembled. Greville
made a quick round of the room, ostentatiously greeting us, and when he reached me he clasped my hand
with his usual reluctant warmth.

"Tia, how are you?" His brown cheeks wrinkled
into a grimace of welcome.

"Well. And yourself?"

He dropped my hand as quickly as he could without being impolite. "Busy, busy as always. Benito,
hello." He didn't offer to take Benito's hand.

Benito growled something and Greville sailed back
to the business end of the bridge, all scientific serious-
ness. Greville had decided to become a scientist-
explorer at about the time I had come back from
Mars, and having been through all the courses, he
had adopted the scientific mien until he grew to become the mask, and the mask had become him. He
affected glasses, rimless circles riding on his nose, and
dyed his bush of black hair white along the temples,
so that his head had the appearance of a tumbleweed
stricken with disease. Frightfully earnest, prissy, neat
to the point of obsession, he spent each voyage giving
"pep" talks and plotting our course, directing each
dive from his safe nest on the bridge of the *Ilium,* and
generally acting as he believed the head of a great
scientific expedition should act. And, indeed, if there
was anything scientific in the least connected with
the *Ilium*'s explorations, it rested on Greville's self-
enamored shoulders. I could see him a century hence,
unless he decided to trade his "science" for something
else, just as earnestly plotting and explaining a dive
into the depths of the Jovian atmosphere. Greville
knew what we were after, but didn't feel what we
were after, and the magic of the enterprise held no
place in his calculations.

"Ahem," Greville began. "Good morning. I'm very
pleased to see you all aboard and ready for our third

voyage to the sunken islands of Hawaii. I believe you all know each other, including our two guests on this trip, Paul Ambuhl and Jenny Crane. Yes. We trust that this voyage will prove both educational and entertaining. Well. Um. Here is a map of the northern Pacific Ocean, and we are here, yes, over the Greater Coastal Bank, directly over what our guests may not realize was once the westernmost edge of the North American continent. California? Um? Yes. We are headed here, down toward the sunken chain of the Hawaiian Islands, and during this trip we are planning to explore the ruins of what was once the largest island of the chain, Hawaii itself. The Hawaiian Islands, once the playground of the North American people, were constantly bathed in warm winds and the warm ocean and so rich that no systematized food production was ever necessary. The islands were populated by a gentle, brown-skinned race who spent their time playing music and riding the waves on planks of wood. They were the inventors, as it so happens, of the modern sport of water-skiing."

Greville paused to let this sink in, oblivious to the fraudulence of his claim. Having reaped a reward of surprised smiles and nods, he continued. "The Hawaiians declined Americanization and remained until the end primitive, untutored, and happy. They had a complicated religion based on the consumption of alcoholic beverages and worshipped their deities through dancing. Their sexual prowess was legendary. Um. Yes. There are various interesting artifacts on these islands, which survived the sinking of part of the chain during the Great Shaping, and it is these ruins which we are exploring and cataloging for the, uh, greater enlightenment of mankind."

More of the same poured forth for another fifteen minutes, much of it fanciful, much of it simply wrong, all of it memorized and delivered in a sleep-inducing monotone. Benito slouched and glowered, and I shared his disgust, though for different reasons. To Greville, to Harkness, to all the rest, the *Ilium* was a toy, a hobby. Each had happened upon the ship, been delighted, created a position and moved in, and when they tired of it they would move on again, perhaps leaving behind a new minaret or balcony, a new dial on the bridge, some scratchings in the archaic logs that someone else had left behind. But to Benito the ship was home and heaven both, and it pained him to see the *Ilium* in the hands of those who did not understand her. And me? To me the *Ilium* was a means of slipping into the amniotic center of the seas, for moving backward in time, five centuries or more, to where I belonged. And, in addition, it pained me to hear nonsense concerning the time I considered my proper home.

Greville finally yielded the floor to the captain, and Harkness briskly charted our voyage, his pseudo-military brevity a relief after Greville's oration. He announced our estimated time of arrival as one week hence, pinpointed the area where the *Ilium* would make her descent and closed the meeting. Paul immediately stood and began making his way toward me, but was intercepted by Greville and the two novices were led away to the museum. Benito stood and slouched from the room. I hesitated for a moment, then caught Tobias' more than normally hateful, knowing glare, and followed Benito's hunched and ugly back down to the generator room.

20

Hunchbacked ugly Benito.

Has a scar where they removed the harelip.

Was conceived on a bet and borne on a bet and born on a bet.

Was abandoned by his loving mommy when they pulled him squawling from between her legs, ass first: male, pink, loud, healthy, hunchbacked, harelipped —the result of conception on a gamble, of nine months without the benefit of someone who would have peered at samples of amniotic fluid and said, "Lady, get rid of it."

Was raised by a nurse from the hospital, a man who wanted children but could not bring himself to enter into a relationship with any other human at all. Who refused to let them fix Benito's back while there was still time, finding the deformities of his own soul in the twisted spine of his adoptive son.

Hunchbacked, ugly Benito Principe, raised in solitude, discovered his difference at the age of eighteen, when his adoptive father kicked him out of the secluded house in which Benito had spent his life. He was given a ticket to the Treatment Center and told never to return, for he had entered the forbidden realm of maturity, and exited the realm of his parent's affections. Benito had been carefully taught not to trust others; now, he was given concrete lessons in the truth behind the teaching. Benito did not hide himself in Australia. Benito hid himself in machines.

He spent hours in the generator hold, checking the lines, monitoring, fixing, polishing, loving the monsters in the bowels of the *Ilium*. Coming up from the hold only when he had to, and disappearing back into it as soon as he could.

Benito found me repulsive and I found him repulsive, and so we tolerated each other, two freaks nestled in the belly of Eden. He was worse off, I told him, because he would have an eternity of bearing his hunchback, no respite. I was worse off, he told me, because I would have to die, and dying was worse than living in any condition. We each suspected the other to be right and remained suspended between superiority on the right, inferiority on the left, the dislike of others above us, and the changeable sea below.

⚜ 21 ⚜

One evening a month after my flight from the Library I called Greg Hartfeld. I'd spent the day in the viewing chamber, gazing out at the bleak and forbidding surface of the moon, and the bareness had swept my mind clear of the last cobwebs. I was going to die. Very well, then, I would spend such time as I was given enjoying, exploring, experiencing. My small apartment began to cramp me, I could hear the emptiness of my days echoing around my skull, and it suddenly seemed a great waste to spend the precious hours of my life parsing my own elegy.

The comsystem shunted my call halfway around the surface of the moon to Clarke Observatory, and soon the round face and hawk nose of Greg Hartfeld filled the screen before me.

"Hi," I said. "Remember me? Tia Hamley?"

"Sure." He laughed. "Sure, of course. You want to walk around on the moon, eh? I'll come to get you, unless you want to come yourself. Today? This evening? Takes an hour and a half, if you leave now you'll be here in time for dinner. Okay?"

"Sure. I'll come by myself."

"Great! You want Clarke Station One. I'll be waiting, catch the sixteen-ten, bring a change of clothes and a toothbrush. Good! I'll see you soon."

I closed the connection, both amused and excited, threw some clothes into a bag, and soared across Luna to the station. I barely caught the sixteen-ten and tumbled out ninety minutes later into Hartfeld's enormous arms.

He swept me along as though I were a child, scattering robo-porters around him like so much dust, talking continuously. We danced and leaped over slidebelts, shot up the lift-tube of a building at the edge of the permasteel bubble, and Greg Hartfeld threw open a door.

"There it is!" he announced, flinging my bag toward a wall. It was caught in the light green aura of a fieldchair. "It is nice, eh? Also cheap, nobody wants to live on the edge of the bubble except nuts like me. They think maybe the moon will sneak in the window some night and gobble them up. And they're right! Look!" He twisted a knob and a holopainting across the room melted into a clear screen. There sat the dry white surface of the moon, etched with black where the slowly setting sun caught the rocks and threw impenetrable shadows.

"Something, eh? Tomorrow we will be out on it, playing gnats on top of the old grave. She will not mind, no, as long as we play by the rules."

I stared at the harshness and felt a great excitement mounting within me. Hartfeld, seeing my concentration, was silent. A sterile eternity, just within the reach of my fingertips, unblemished by the great green orb of Earth. Not a landscape of death, no more than it was a landscape of life; it transcended both, transcended mortality and immortality. In that monochromatic stillness, my problems were totally irrelevant, and ceased to exist. I forgot to breathe and put my fingertips against the screen in awe and supplication. The viewing chambers of Luna, with their labeled vistas and crowded comforts, had not prepared me for anything like this.

"She is a real bitch," Hartfeld said finally.

"But beautiful," I replied.

"You think so?" he said with great interest, and the spell of the moon burst. "Well, we shall see tomorrow, eh? You are hungry, take a bath, change your clothes, you always wear clothes? No matter, we'll go out and eat lots, and you'll meet some more nuts, just like me. We collect 'em up here, maybe you'll fit in, maybe not. There's the bathroom, you like water showers? Okay, you get four gallons hot, ten cold— you know that already, I am a fool. Punch your number into the wall, the machine'll turn on if you're allowed the water. We gotta keep tight control up here, not like old lady Earth, eh? Good!"

The evening took on the flavor of Greg Hartfeld, massive, exuberant, unceasing, bewildering. We dined in a small, richly scented restaurant, where four people waited for us at a corner table. "Other nuts," Greg called them, but none so large or overpowering as him. The conversation glittered, not with the usual Immortal collection of dusty injokes and borrowed opinions, but with theses, arguments, counterarguments; observations, analysis. Life, to these people, seemed a labyrinth of infinite fascination, and I, fascinated in turn, spun and bobbed in their wake, enchanted. Dinner finished, we talked our way to someone's apartment, also tucked into the edge of the bubble. With the harsh moonscape as background, dark Najla talked of astrophysics and the history of the Minoan empire; Greg argued with tiny Susan about life-support systems, bare seconds after an argument with Kai-Yu over communications techniques; Jaime sang softly and softly commented on Najla's theories. Once, in the course of a discussion on art, I diffidently offered a quotation I had picked up dur-

ing my time at the library, and Greg enveloped me
in a bear hug and crowed. Embarrassed and pleased,
I retreated to silence again. My god, but these people were alive! Closing my eyes against the room,
against the moon, listening to the rush and tumult of
their conversation, I could believe that I had slipped
into the past, into a time where ideas were new, con-
cepts were fresh, where things mattered, where time
mattered. Someone passed around more dope, someone talked about hydroponics. These people, I thought
suddenly, were as different from mainstream Immortal culture as were the desperate freaks of
Australia, but when I tried to follow the thought it
skipped away from me. I yawned.

When we finally left, as the night-glow of the dome
was slowly diffusing into a programmed dawn, I was
still too stoned and too sleepy to cope with the light
gravity. Greg wrapped an arm around me to keep
me from swaying off the slidebelt.

"We drown you a little, eh?" he said as we entered
his apartment.

"Yes," I admitted. "Maybe I was too high to make
sense of it— Greg? Have you ever been to Australia?"

He held my shoulders and smiled down at me.
"Strange little bird, what made you think that?"

"I don't know." I smiled back at him. "I'm too tired
to think. Where do I sleep?"

"With me? I would like to make love with you, little bird. If you wish."

I briefly considered my slight fear of him, of his
size and his mind, and briefly considered Paul, and
thought of the Library of the Moon, and smiled and
nodded and moved toward him.

It was spectacularly good.

22

The *Ilium* moved through gentle seas, through sunsets and sunrises and the moon at night, through phosphorescent water punctuated by shimmers of light. The haze of land dropped away beneath us, the cries of birds circling our minarets became fewer, and the ocean took us on faith, as she had taken so many on faith; we rode her breathing skin toward the west and toward the south.

Greville plotted his dives, gave his pep-talks, made sure to come around to each one of us at least once a day to chat, elucidate, bother and annoy. Harkness, as usual, spent most of his time on the bridge, pounding his body into the military trim he felt fitting to his role, or playing quadrachess with sweet, delicate Hart. Li created and ate concoctions in the kitchen when he wasn't sleeping, screwing with Lonnie, or taking his shift in the control bridge. Lonnie, seeming unaffected by Li's corpulent mass moving nightly above her,

arched over her tri-boards, shaping new minarets with
movements of her brown fingertips, with hunchings of
her sharp eyebrows. Tobias divided his time between
the engine room and the diving hold, Jenny always
close behind him. Benito kept to the humming cloister
of his generators. Paul had asked for a reassignment
from Jenny's room, had moved out a bare ten minutes before Tobias moved in. I took Paul with me to
the generator room once or twice, but Benito's scowl
and ugliness put him off, and he would soon make
excuses to leave us while he wandered about the intricate mazes of the ship.

Mist-voyage. Dream-trip, half in and half out of
reality, those first five days at sea, as the land fell
away and was swallowed up by the grey-green waters.
Like any dream-trip it had small tensions within it,
the edges of nightmare slicing like hard, bright wires
stretched taut through the fabric of days. Jenny and
Tobias kept to themselves, left rooms as I entered
them; Paul reported that they did the same to him.
Benito was more than usually sullen, Greville poured
forth more than his usual good cheer. The others, ill
at ease, avoided Paul or me or both of us together. I
sensed a heightening of the reactions usually present
around me; felt a suspicion that the shock which had
tumbled forth from Jenny, days and leagues ago by
the side of the sea, also troubled the other voyagers.
I shunted it off to an unused corner of my consciousness, wrapped it tight for storage, buried it in unexpected happiness.

I did not let it bother me that I shut off half of my
mind to be with Paul, that he was a child, shallow, a
fool. An Immortal and immortally vain. Yes, all of
that, but still the man who swung with me in my hammock or who cradled me in the warmth of his bed,
who kissed my neglected breasts to life again. I did
not know why he did these things and did not worry
at my lack of knowledge, did not want to know. It
was enough that he held me and spoke to me and

awakened me in the mornings with soft words and sudden, ecstatic penetrations.

As for the others, I ignored them. Life had given me few enough rainbows; I would not let their hatreds and horrors wrench this one, final rainbow away. Like shadows, they floated beyond the boundaries of my new universe, and I had no wish to let them in.

23

I had moved into Greg Hartfeld's apartment three days after arriving at Clarke, when we'd both decided that I would be around for a while, and I took a job as a linewalker with the transport company. Once a week Greg and I went out, followed by remotes and carriers, and walked the line, patching patches, refusing the tough plasteel until no seams showed at all. Once a week we walked the inside of the tube, once a week we did long-range surveys in the hopper, and once a week we caught up with the paperwork. Every two weeks the company transferred our substantial wages from its account to ours—the company paid well, and we received hazardous duty allowances when we walked the line. My stipend from the Treatment Center accumulated quietly in my separate account at Berne; I had not, and would not, tell Greg about it, or about the reason for it, and that secret was the only disjunctive note in our life together.

Sharing our jobs, our home, our bodies, had created a bond between us which I, at times, equated to an Ancient passion; the drive to grant one's lover the surrogate immortality of verse or sculpture, prose or painting. Beside Greg, the sparkling chambers of Venice became, in memory, a children's amusement park, and what passion I had felt for Paul paled. Greg was an unending reservoir of strength, of excitement; even at his most annoying (and he could, at times, be astonishingly annoying), I could not conceive of being elsewhere.

We spent much of our free time in the company of Greg's friends, and my initial impressions of them had not changed. They seemed alive in ways I had never experienced, as though they had effected a blending of cultures, using immortality not as an endpoint, a goal, but as a springboard for change. They shared much of my own growing discomfort with the Immortal way of life, and they provided charts and graphs by the ream, showing the decline of invention over the past five centuries, the decline in art and music, in exploration and curiosity, in science and mathematics. The Immortals, said Najla with disgust, had taken the most important advance in history and used it to stop advancement forever; the Immortals accepted their static world, but these people did not.

My initial, instinctive connection between Greg and his friends, and Australia, eventually clarified: they were the opposite ends of a scale, alike in their dissatisfaction with the Immortal mainstream of the mid-scale, antithetical in their expressions of that dislike. The freaks of Australia lacked cohesiveness, but in the society at Clarke I sensed a core, a purpose, that I had never felt before.

After three months at Clarke that core was finally shown to me. Greg and his friends scooped me up as I entered the dome at the end of an exhausting day walking the line, brought me to a shadowed ravine kilometers away from the observatory, and showed me the center of their dreams. They had a ship, a

slim, burnished line of metal whose tip caught the
light and gleamed unbearably bright. They talked
at me for two hours, leading me from one end of the
vessel to the other, showing me charts and diagrams,
life-support systems, bunks, mess-halls, drives, rec-
reation areas, hydroponic gardens, baths, control
rooms, medical centers, workshops, until my initial
wonderment faded to confusion, and I begged for one
hour's peace to assimilate it all.

Kind, understanding, confident, they loaned me a
Barré suit, and I scrabbled up the sides of the ravine
until I found an escarpment of rock to sit on, legs dangling and heels kicking idly at the lunar stone. The
warmth of the deceptively flimsy-looking suit encased
me, just as the repellor fields encased the slim ship in
the valley below me.

The ship was called the *Outbound*. They were
planning to launch it within five years, couple it with
the circular disc that orbited, almost finished, around
the pole, so that the ship would resemble a shaft of
gold driven through a silver plate. Then they would
aim it toward the sun, whip around the skirts of Sol,
and use the borrowed momentum to fling the ship,
and themselves, into interstellar space. They would
float gravely through the void, rotating about the longi-
tudinal axis of the ship, until they found a habitable
planet and could set up housekeeping far from Mother
Terra. But, they explained to me, once launched there
would be no hurry; if the first planet didn't work out
they would look for another, and another, no need to
rush. They were Immortals, after all. They could
take their time.

And they wanted me to go with them.

I kicked at the rock a bit harder. A piece cracked
away and wafted down the face of the cliff to the floor
of the valley. The Immortals congregated in their ship,
confident that I would come bounding down the hill
with a ready acceptance on my lips, eager as they
were to finish up, to prepare, to catapult myself into

the unknown with them. But I was not at all sure that
I wanted to go.

It wasn't their philosophy that stopped me. They
weren't fleeing an imagined persecution directed
against some preposterous belief, they weren't depart-
ing to bring Truth or Right or Good to the benighted
aliens circling some distant sun. They were, simply,
planning to create a society that preserved the benefits
of Immortality while nurturing the spirit and drive
extant before the Great Shaping. I agreed with their
belief that the society they envisioned would find no
haven on Terra; fads among the Immortals were violently accepted and, sucked dry, entirely rejected, and
even the most cohesive of groups could not long survive under the insistent curiosity of the culture around
them. Nor did I object to the members of the group.
I had no doubt that I would continue to enjoy the
company of Kai-Yu and Susan, Najla and Jaime, or
the other, yet unknown members who were scattered
over the Earth and her two outposts, working toward
the launching of their dream. Least of all would I tire
of the company of Greg. But I loved him, and it was
love that stopped me from crying a ready acceptance
to a voyage to the stars.

I was twenty-one years old. My face and body still
bore a bloom consistent with Immortality, and had
the Treatments worked I would look like that forever.
But I had studied in the dim quiet of the Library and
carefully created a chronology for myself. I would live,
with luck, to see my two-hundredth birthday. The
mortals of before the Shaping lived, with luck, for
ninety years. At two hundred I would be shriveled
and tucked, seamed and weak and lined and dithering.
At one hundred I would be caught between that state
and the next one down, between middle-age and senil-
ity. At seventy-five I would be just beyond prime—hair
greying, lines on face and body, mind quick and ready,
eyes bright. At fifty I would be well into maturity,
with small crinkles growing along the corners of my
eyes. The ancient mortals had thought a woman of

forty capable of great beauty; Lippencott's Children
had never seen anyone looking that age, and would
find me hideous. As I would find myself hideous.

As I died somewhere between the stars, Greg would
look exactly as he had that morning, rising naked
from our tumbled bed. They would all of them be
unchanged as I withered and drooled and, eventually,
died.

I kicked a boulder and it, too, floated toward the
valley, lifting a trail of pale dust behind it. It rocked
itself to a stop forty meters from the ship, well before
it reached the protective field. I stretched out on my
stomach and gazed through the haze of dust at the
distant horizon. Earth lay over the ridge of mountains,
perpetually out of sight.

Earth. Mother Terra. Home. Earth would brand
me with my separateness as soon as my face branded
itself. I searched my soul and felt not the least quiver
of love for the planet of my birth, felt only an abyss
that promised, with time, to fill with hatred. To stay
on Earth was to be constantly surrounded by the
frigid dislike of others, was to be apart and alone—as
alone as I would be if I ventured between the stars.
A difference in quantity if not in quality and, perhaps,
even a difference there. By the time my body betrayed
me into age, the company of the *Outbound* would know
me; would, perhaps, love me; would understand and
accept me as those indifferent populations below could
never do.

And if they wouldn't? But they would have to, they
would have no choice. No turning back, no marooning
me on some deserted interstellar island. They would
do a health check on me, for form's sake. Well, let
them. My anomaly wouldn't turn up on their ordinary
tests, and no one demanded a Certificate of Immortality in a world where everyone was immortal. Nor
could they obtain records of my Treatment without
my permission, a permission I was not likely to grant.
They wanted children: well, so did I, and perhaps,
beyond the stars, their need for children would allow

them to reverse what had been done to me, and my
loneliness would be, again, mitigated. So I would
leave with them, the worm of time tucked within me
like a stowaway, and when that stowaway was discovered it would be too late for anything but acceptance.

And love? The torture of seeing a loved one wither
to dust? I did not wish it on Greg but, I decided as I
stood, neither did I wish it on myself. Surely a little
selfishness was understandable. And he would have
our child, our children, long after I had gone; it
seemed an appropriately Ancient form of immortality
for this group of inappropriately ancient Immortals.
Here and now, I told myself, and let the future look
to itself.

I shook the dust from the invisible folds of the Barré
suit and bounded down the side of the hill toward the
waiting ship.

24

I sat in the vast quiet of the generator hold while Benito played with a confusion of tiny parts spread out on his workbench. He carefully fit small gears onto small shafts, small belts over small drives, holding things together with microscopic pins and screws. Benito was making a sculpture. I didn't know if he knew it or not, but sculpture indeed was beneath his splayed fingers. He had been building this small machine when I first met him, three years ago, and was still working on it with infinite patience. The only times he was content, it seemed to me, were during those long, slow, silent sessions at his workbench while he built his toy.

Around us the generators hummed so quietly as to be just on the edge of perception. Each was encased in its shining metal plates, separated by clean walkways. They extended from where we sat near the middle of the hold for the entire length and breadth

of the *Ilium;* the furthest reaches were but dim glows
and the humming seemed a condition of the air. The
workdesk and its adjacent control console created a
semi-circle resting on a circular platform; the platform
moved constantly, slowly, making a complete turn
every half-hour, and the regiments of gleaming bronze
and silver generators marched before us.

I sat sprawled in a field chair, relaxed enough in
Benito's sighing cloister to be as ungainly as I wished,
with a calibrator almost forgotten in my lap and the
pulser on which I was working resting quiet on the
floor before me. Illuminated on the screen of my eyelids, I saw the *Outbound* resting in her cradle dark-
side, and a second later saw her moving through space,
connected to her halo, vanes extended, spinning slowly
against a backdrop of stars. It was not an image that
I returned to readily, but one that pounced on my
unsuspecting mind during such moments as these and
left me with a sense of shame, of longing coupled
with burning curiosity. Someone, something was
picking up the reports the *Outbound* broadcast every
ship's week, but I had not tried to find out who or
what was doing the monitoring. To know of the *Outbound* was sufficient, to know about the *Outbound*
would be both useless and painful. I played games
beneath the cover of my eyelids instead, speculating
uselessly and painfully in the breathing silence of the
huge chamber.

"This Paul is an ass," Benito said suddenly.

Startled, I opened my eyes. He remained hunched
over his workbench and for a moment I thought I had
imagined the words.

"An ass," he repeated, and put down the small
pliers. He turned to face me, his usual scowl shifted
slightly into the combative.

"Why?"

"Why? You're an ass too, if you don't see it."

"I see it," I said after a slight pause. "I know what
he is." Benito looked skeptical. "All right, he's a child,

he's selfish, he's shallow, he's a coward like all of them. . . ."

"And he fucks you."

"Okay, he fucks me, we do it to each other, so what?"

"To each other?"

"Perish, Benito, what's your problem?"

"I have no problems, I am completely normal!" He rose and stormed around the semi-circle, his hump moving as he waved his arms. "You think that because I have this on my back, I have it over my eyes, too? I'm not blind, Tia."

"What in the hell are you talking about?"

"Look, why do you think someone goes to bed with a hunchback, with me? Why?"

I had no answer, so said nothing.

"I'll tell you why, then. Because it's perverse, because they aren't fucking with me, no, just with this thing on my back. Understand?"

"So?"

"So?" he mimicked viciously. "You think maybe I've got a monopoly on hideousness?"

"Balls, Benito."

"Okay, so this Paul, this wonderchild—listen, old hag, who do you think he's shoving into when he shoves between your legs? You think he's pronging Tia Hamley? If you believe that, you're stupid, *stupid!*

"Shut up! Benito, this is probably the last time, do you understand? The very last time, don't kill it for me."

"Stupid!"

"Why are you so worried, anyway? What's it to you?"

"Because we're the twisted ones, you and I," he hissed. "Bear the full weight of it, Tia. All the pain, all of it, no delusions, no masks."

"Hell, Benito, you're just jealous, is all."

"Jealous?" he hooted.

"Sure. You couldn't even get it up, remember?"

The sting of saying it equalled the sting of receiving it, and we both gasped.

"Jesus, Benito, I'm sorry. . . ."

"You bitch," he spat.

"Benito. . . ."

"You've got your brains between your legs, just like the rest of them!"

I threw the calibrator down on the chair and hopped over the edge of the revolving platform. "Just let it ride, will you?"

"You in love with him, Tia?" Benito shouted.

"Shut up!" I yelled back as I paced through the gleaming generators.

"He make you feel young again?"

"Shut up!"

"What's the flavor of old cunt, Tia?"

"SHUT UP!"

"Does he leave the lights on?"

"*Shut the death up!*" I screamed and slammed the heavy door behind me. Through the thick panelling I could hear reverberating shouts, but whether they were new insults from Benito or only the echoes of our screams I could not tell.

I forced myself to walk slowly down the corridors of the *Ilium,* up the lift tubes, through arching colonnades and up twisting archaic staircases that clung to the side of the ship, until I reached one of the vacant minarets. The onion-shaped crystal room atop it would eventually be used for astrogation, but now it was clean, quiet, and abandoned. I stared from the window, watching the foam created by our passing flow from the stern, to my right. We were moving slowly toward the southwest, barely resting on the skin of the ocean; the last land had dropped over the edge of the world days ago. We could have lifted the entire ship and been over the Islands an hour after leaving shore, but there was no hurry, never any hurry aboard a ship with eternity to waste. So the ocean stretched before and behind us, foam glistened in our wake, and the sun sent evening shafts of light through the stained

glass in the windows behind me, dappled the marble
floor in wine-rich hues. The wind was warm and sweet.

"You in love with him, Tia?" Love? With Paul?
No, of course not. Nothing of the stoppage of breath
and words, the sudden falterings of the soul, the arteries of blinding and illuminating fire that I had experienced with Greg. True, there was one thing in
common; with neither had I felt the furious longing of
the heart when my lover was not with me, the emptiness that accompanied separation. But with Greg, until
those last months, my serenity had been the absolute
confidence of togetherness, the knowledge that the
separations, however slight, however long, were tem-
porary, that the hearts and souls held firm. No need
to fear. And, with Paul, the confidence was simply the
result of, if not indifference, at least not deep passion.
I had loved Greg, needed Greg, and the need had not
threatened me. I did not love Paul, for how could one
love an alien? And the need, therefore, did not exist.

Yet I did no justice to the situation by dismissing it
so easily, by neatly boxing and labeling the emotions
and hoping that they would thenceforward behave
themselves and cause me no more trouble. There were
needs and desires in this curious relationship, some of
which I had resolutely decided not to pursue. Why did
Paul lie with me? Desire me? There could be no simple physical attraction behind his midnight urgencies,
not surrounded as he was with the physical beauty of
Jenny or Lonnie, or, for that matter, of Tobias. Darkness seemed to rise behind the question, and I side-
stepped, knowing as I supplied the easy answer that
the question had not been met. Paul was, simply, fond
of me, remembered Venice, perhaps even felt sorry
for me, but I did not pursue the thought. After all, it
was not so much Paul's feelings that mattered as my
own, I assured myself, and the assurance in itself was
guarantee of a lack of love. Paul *was* my final rainbow, my last grab at something approximating normal-
ity, of something close to joy. Or he was, perhaps, only
the simple meeting of a physical need. I had been

celibate for seven years before Paul and expected, once he left, to be celibate for the rest of my short life. That, I decided, was reason enough to run from the unmitigated pain of difference that Benito offered, the unsoftened knowledge of freakery and death. For the knowledge and the pain would have their due; nights would be sleepless and days spent in crowded loneliness. There would be many opportunities to pay for the sins of my strangeness. Time for a hundred visions and revisions, but not yet. Not yet.

The rays of the sun slanted almost horizontally across the round chamber, and I twisted my hair more tightly behind my head and went to mess.

Benito sat at one end of the oval table, Paul slightly down from him and across, and a vacant place beside each of them. Without hesitation, I crossed the patterned tile floor and sat beside Paul, and Benito refused to look at me.

25

Five days from land. The deep belly-thrumming of the generators told me that we were changing course, and I sat on one of the ledges of my minaret, watching the bow of the *Ilium* carve long triangles into the sea. Paul had found a book on yoga in my personal library and was locked in his cabin, trying to tie his legs into knots. Tobias had decided to spend the day in the museum, while Harkness and Greville argued over the holocharts in the bridge. There was but one place where I was sure not to be interrupted, and there I sat, high above the flight deck and on the other side of the minaret from it, legs dangling between the wrought-iron rail supports, over the white-flecked waters.

"Uh, excuse me."

I turned and squinted up at Jenny. She stood near the wall, arms loose at her sides and fingers twitching against her browned thighs. "May I join you?"

"Sure." I gestured toward a place by the ledge, and

she sat cautiously, legs wrapped around one of the rail supports. She grasped the rail and leaned forward, looked down at the moving blue below us, then gasped and pointed.

"Look! What are those?"

I glanced at the bow, where sleek dark shapes capered.

"Dolphins. They often ride with us, pure sport, I guess."

"I read in an old book once that they're intelligent, that they talk to each other."

I shrugged. "Yes, and probably the same's true of whales. But research stopped during the Shaping, and no one's taken it up again."

"Pity," she said and leaned back to catch the sunlight full on her face. Her thick, black hair swept the deck behind her, brushed across the knuckles of her pulled-back hands. I sat quietly, waiting for her to speak, but she too kept a long silence. A seagull mewed plaintively, and the generators thrummed as we held steady on the new course.

"Tia?"

"Um?"

"What's it, well, I mean. . . ."

I turned to look at her. "What is it, Jenny?"

She laughed nervously, played with her hair. "I'm a little scared of mentioning it. I mean, I don't want to offend you."

"Oh? Why don't you just ask, and then if I'm offended I won't answer, okay?"

"Well, what does it feel like? Being old, I mean? There, I told you you'd be offended."

"Jenny, how old are you?"

She looked startled, frowned a moment, then said, "A hundred ten. I think. It's sort of hard to keep track."

"And I'm sixty-seven years, eight months, fourteen days, and um, about eleven hours. So you're considerably older than I. You'd be better fitted to answer your own questions."

"That's not what I meant."

"I know, I know." I leaned my forearms against the low railing, rested chin on wrists. "It's not something I like talking about."

Pause. "Are you very lonely?"

I didn't answer that. After a moment, Jenny continued.

"I mean, are there any others like you?"

"I used to hope so. I used to look for someone. I'd have heard, or my doctors would have heard. No, there's no one like me, Jenny. Do you find that a relief?"

This time, she didn't answer.

"I wanted children, once," I said, mostly to the dolphins. "Maybe selfishly, so there could be others like me. But I didn't. One gets used to it, after a while."

"Really?"

"No."

I heard her moving slightly.

"Does it hurt?" she said.

"Sometimes. Some things."

"Like?"

I turned to her, my cheek against my arms. "Aren't you being a bit morbid?"

She flushed, moved her hands defensively. "I'm not trying to pry. It's—it's not for me."

"Then the others can ask their own questions, can't they?" I said harshly, and went back to watching the dolphins. But she didn't go away, and when I glanced at her from the corner of my eye, she, too, was leaning on crossed wrists watching the cavorting shapes ahead of us.

"Tobias is very moody, isn't he?" she asked unexpectedly.

"I suppose."

"Do you know why?"

"Why should I? He does his job, I do mine."

"But you spend so much time together, during the dives and like that."

"He does his job, I do mine. He's not particularly fond of me."

"Well, you're not too friendly, either," she said with a touch of heat.

"Am I expected to be? He goes out of his way to show me what he thinks of me. There's no law that says I have to love my detester."

"It's not hate," she began.

"No? Then it's something pretty damned close. I have enough to worry about, without that."

"It's not hate," she said again. "It's. . . ." and she bit her lip. Another silence ensued.

"How long were you with Paul?" I asked, and to my satisfaction, she looked uncomfortable.

"About three years."

"Yes? Did you enjoy him?"

She shook her head, in confusion rather than negation. "Paul's . . . odd," she said slowly. "No, I didn't enjoy him, not always. But I think I understand him better now."

"Are you still angry with him?"

"For what?"

"Me."

Again the confused shake of the head, and a disturbed creasing around the eyes. "I don't know, I'm not sure. I'm, things are so, so changing. I just don't know anymore." Her shoulders shivered, swiftly and suddenly. "Paul has bad dreams."

"Bad dreams? What kind?"

But she was already standing. "Look, I promised Tobias I'd be back before mess-time. I've really got to go. Thanks for talking with me."

"Sure. Come again," I said, then Jenny leaned forward quickly, brushed my cheek with her fingertips, and ran like hell down the stairs, leaving me staring after her in amazement.

26

"Yes, but is it safe?" Paul asked for the fourth time that afternoon.

I cursed myself for an idiot and began putting away the bits of my wet-suit that lay scattered on the multi-colored mosaic floor of the first level of the diving hold. "If you use the slightest amount of common sense, it's as safe as a bubble-suit," I replied again.

He nodded shortly, unconvinced, and fingered the faceplate before handing it to me. "Why don't you show me the bubble-suits now?" he asked.

Subject closed. I had, for some reason, been hoping that I could talk him into wet-suiting with me, but his response had been an impenetrable lack of interest, coupled with an absolute refusal to consider my assurances that wet-suiting wouldn't kill him. Well, we would dive in two more days; he, Jenny and Tobias in bubble-suits and I in my wet-suit, and that would be that. So be it. I finished layering my equipment in the storage chamber, irised the mouth closed and led the way along the circular rim of the first level to the bubble-suits.

"You've used one of these before," I began, and waited for his nod. "All right, then, here's the shunts, you'll notice that they're a bit different from those you're used to; greater generation to offset the greater depths you'll be in. Air recycler, radio, stabilizers so that you don't go turning end for end. The propulsion equipment operates out of the main generator. It's modified standard. Radiates from this and this, here on the waistband. So the centerpoint of the field is really the centerpoint of you, and the rim will always remain the same distance from you. Remember that you won't be able to touch the walls once the field is operating. Controls for the remotes here, on wristbands, sight and sound on the right, motion on the left, it'll take you about five minutes to get used to them, they're fairly straightforward. Screen hangs from the waist-belt, so. The equipment sac rides in the bubble with you, here, and there's a tricky bit of electronics to keep it from penetrating the bubble wall, or bashing into you during turbulence." I held the equipment sac in my palm and turned it over a couple of times. "Benito's work," I explained to Paul. "All the modifications. Okay, that's about it."

"What if I get knocked against a building, or some fish tries to get in?"

"Remember that the field is set at no-displacement, like a table or floor, rather than some-displacement, like a chair or bed. Anything that tries to get in will just get bounced away, and if you get too close to something solid you get bounced away, bubble and all."

"Okay. How long's the recycler good for?"

"It'll work as long as the generator batteries last. They're fully charged before a dive, so even with full use you won't get a complete drain for about twenty-six or twenty-eight hours. But you won't be under that long."

"And if I get stuck somewhere?" He looked very worried, and I could hear the sharpness of my impatience in my voice.

"See this? It's a homing call. Your position is on the bridge screen at all times, so there's no danger that you might get stuck and not be rescued in time. If the rescue takes longer than you're charged for, we simply build a second bubble around the first one, pump in air, and you deactivate your field and use the larger one."

"So it's just about perfectly safe?" Paul asked.

"Perfectly safe," I agreed. He ignored the bite in my tone and inspected the bubble-suit equipment happily.

The intercom burped suddenly and Harkness' voice filled the hold.

"Attention. All crew to bridge immediately. Attention."

I turned, sprinted across the diving hold, and was on my way up the dropshaft with Paul close behind me before Harkness issued his command again.

"Does that mean me, too?" Paul asked as we ascended.

"Sure, honorary."

"What's going on?"

"Don't know," I replied. I jumped a floater and scooted down the hall toward a second shaft. The last time an alert had been called, Greville had discovered a dolphin in the diving well and had raised an unholy commotion until I slipped into my suit and guided the creature back to the open sea. But Harkness had called this alert, and it was Harkness who stood near the control banks, watching the crew enter the room, while Greville stood shouting at Benito. The chief engineer slouched scowling, hands balled against his thighs, seemingly oblivious to Greville's tirade.

"I'll bet it's the generators," Lonnie said quietly to Paul as he entered behind me. "I heard Benito growling at them this morning during my shift."

I felt a slight sting. I was the one who usually knew,

first after Benito, of the workings of the generator
room. But I hadn't been down since our argument
and Benito had certainly not sought me out to invite
me.

Li, late as usual, entered in a quivering rush, and
Greville advanced to his "leader of the expedition"
post.

"Ahem," he began. "Benito tells me that we have
a problem with the generators. There is no need to
panic, no. Ahem. Yes. Benito says that one of the
generators is, uh, malfunctioning. The *Ilium* will not
be able to dive. Ahem." He looked about him, lost
without a prepared speech. Benito, still slouched
against the control bank, began speaking.

"Look, the number fourteen starboard generator is
acting funny. If we go down, the load is too much
and we leak at that sector, no good. But we're fine as
long as we stay on the surface. I can fix the generator
in four or five days—maybe I'll need new parts and
that might take longer, I don't know yet. I told Greville, Greville wants to go home."

"No," I said.

"No, that is what I think," Benito agreed. "We are
safe here. They can dive from the surface, that is no
problem, nothing new."

"I say we vote," Greville announced. "Can I see a
show of hands? Return to the mainland?"

"Hold it, Greville, we haven't discussed this yet,"
Harkness interrupted. He strode to the map screen,
lofted a pointer and thwacked against the images behind him as he spoke. "I think Benito's right. We are,
approximately, here, six days out and over the main
island by tomorrow, in place by tomorrow night. The
sea is even, and we're going to be well out from the
Mauna Loa breakers. No storms brewing anywhere
within the Pacific circle. . . ."

"Storms are okay," Benito interrupted. "Just no diving."

"Thank you. Diving from the surface presents no
hazards, it's been done often enough before." Hark-

ness released the pointer and angled his glance around the room. "I would hate to be in command of a ship that turned tail and scooted home at the first sign of trouble. I say we continue."

"I agree," Jenny said. "I'm spending a lot for this trip, and I don't want to go back without diving. If Benito says it's safe, and if Tobias and . . . and Tia say it's safe, then I want to do it."

I nodded thoughtfully at her, remembering my initial liking. "Yes, it's safe enough," I replied. "Your bubble-suits are pressured so that decompression times won't be too long. At the depths we'll be going to, we'll be limited to only one dive a day, but that should pose no problems. It won't be as convenient, of course, as when the *Ilium* dives and we don't have to worry about individual decompression, and we'll have to bring artifacts further to get them in the ship, but these are pretty minor considerations. It should be as safe as diving from below. I say we do it."

"But if one generator blows, the others might, too," Greville protested. "Maybe even the generators in the bubble-suits. I don't think we ought to take the chance."

"No generator has blown," Benito insisted. "My generators do not blow. This is preventative, just to clean this one up, its readings are a bit off. Nothing has blown and nothing is going to blow. You think that maybe it's communicable? No, my generators are fine. Dive."

"Well, I don't know," Hart offered. "I mean, we're all the way out in the middle of the ocean, it's not like being in port. I mean, if something goes, well, it just does, doesn't it? It's a big chance we're taking, I think."

"If you didn't like the risks, you shouldn't have come," Tobias said. "If we're going to dive, then let's dive; if we're going, let's go. This is a waste of time." He crossed his arms, crossed his ankles and slouched down in the chair. His blue eyes glowered about the room and his lower lip, thrust out, barely quivered. Tobias had made his stand, firmly and resolutely right in the middle.

Greville shrugged and called the vote. Hart, Li, and Greville wanted to return to the mainland; Benito, Harkness, Tobias, Jenny, and I wanted to dive. Paul cast his vote at the last minute, for diving, and Lonnie declared that it was all the same to her.

"I can do my work no matter where we are," she explained to Paul, leaning against his shoulder while she looked up at him. "Up, down, here or there. I'm adaptable."

Isn't she just, I thought, and rose. Benito strode from the room, Harkness briskly returned to his controls, and Greville, accompanied by much waving of arms, conversed with Hart and Li.

"Coming?" I asked Paul, and turned without waiting for his answer. He stood quickly and followed me to the diving hold.

"Look, Tia, are you sure this will be safe?" he asked as we dropped.

"I said so, didn't I?"

"Yes, but are you really sure?"

I didn't bother to reply. As I straightened the equipment in my locker, Jenny and Tobias entered the room. They nodded quickly at us and moved toward the bubble-suit equipment where Tobias, with a great show of professionalism, began displaying the stuff to Jenny. As I watched them, I realized that he was playing to me rather than to her, and with great bravado. Ah, beautiful Tobias was not going to be outshone by a withered hag. But Jenny was truly interested and asked endless questions, relevant ones, while Paul played with my airhoses and funked.

27

Li grabbed a handful of bread, mopped enthusiastically at the gravy floating on his plate, and waved the sopping bread to emphasize his point before shoving it into his mouth.

"It's a *good* place to dive," he said again. "All this good stuff, you see. Some places, 'mff, 'cuse me, some places all you get is stuff that breaks apart, but there there's a lot of *good* stuff. And the fishing's great. Hey, Tobias, you gonna bring me some marlin first dive?"

"Sure," Tobias grumbled. "What else do you want? Crab? Lobster? Oysters? Clams? Squid? How about a whale?"

"Hey, you can't get all that stuff 'round here," Li protested genially, and washed down his bread with a great swill of wine.

"Besides, we already have a whale aboard," Lonnie observed, and smiled at both Li and at Paul beside him. "If there's one thing Li knows about diving, it's what kind of fish are where," she told Paul. "He may not know anything else, but he does know fish."

"And don't you appreciate it," Li said.

I sipped the wine, watching Paul return Lonnie's smile, then Li leaned between us and plopped another pastie onto my plate.

"Here, eat, eat," he commanded. "Benito, have some more, there's loads left in the kitchen."

"Galley," Tobias reminded him.

"Galley, kitchen, what-the-hell, have some more."

"Tobias can use them for bait," Lonnie suggested, glancing sideways down the table to where Tobias sat. He ignored her, but Paul smiled.

"What about this good stuff?" Jenny said. "Why are these islands better than, say, California? Or one of the places that sank slowly? Wasn't Hawaii hit by a bunch of tidal waves before it sank?"

"Yes, tsunamis," I said. "But most of them happened during the sinking, not before. The water level rose fairly quickly during the first melt, then the pressure change at the pole activated a lot of the fault lines and the volcanic areas along the Pacific Basin. Mauna Loa really cut loose and covered most of the west side of the island with lava, then the tsunamis generated by other volcanic activity hit. Take a look at the volcano tomorrow; the black cliffs show where the successive tidal waves hit the lava flows—it looks like steps cut into the mountain. What with one thing and another, by the time the last waterwall came down from the pole, most of Hilo, for example, was already under water."

"There are," Greville announced, "some plans to try underwater excavation of the west side of the island, what the natives called the, uh, um, Coffee Side. Of course, it will take considerable equipment and expertise to cut through the layer of, ahem, volcanic rock, and under water, too, to the city below. But we believe that we'll do a creditable job of it."

"If we get the job at all," Harkness said. Greville looked wounded.

"Anyway," I said hastily, "when that last water-wall hit, the waves rolled over Hilo at about ten meters from original sea level, higher in some places due to current formation. In downtown Hilo, you'll see that many of the buildings are sheared off at a certain point, as though they were cut through with some huge laser."

"Of course," Tobias said, "many of the smaller buildings were demolished, completely. No use at all."

"But not all," I said. "Some buildings were protected by other buildings closer to the waterfront, that took the brunt of the waves. And there were some smaller buildings that, quite simply, were well-constructed enough to make it through almost undamaged. This, of course, helps us a lot."

"And the Hawaiians were pretty swift in their use of materials even before the Shaping," Tobias said. He obviously wanted to carry the conversation, so I sat back and let him. "A humid atmosphere. Lots of salt in the air. They had to use things that didn't rot too quickly—plastics, non-corrosive metals, that sort of thing. Kept the stuff in good condition, even under water. Inland places, like under the California Sea, they didn't bother with protecting their things, so you don't find very many valuable artifacts there."

"Iron, for example," Greville said, "simply disintegrates."

"Yes," Tobias began.

"Iron, poof," Hart commented sagely, making tiny explosions with his fingers. "You just touch the stuff and there it goes, like dust."

"Exactly," Greville said.

"Like dust," Lonnie explained, and everyone nodded at everyone else, all agreeing on this basic piece of knowledge.

"But not always," Benito said, his love of machinery outweighing, for the nonce, his dislike for conversation. "You touch the stuff, sure, it crumbles, but you enclose the thing in a bubble, see, and when you bring it up you've gotta keep the pressure constant, consistent with the pressure where you picked the thing up. And be sure to cushion it. One bubble for the thing, another for cushioning, and you got it."

"Of course, you can't get it out again," Greville said.

"Poof," Hart reminded him. "Poof, poof."

"Yes, indeed. Poof." Greville must have caught the amused smile that passed between Hart and Harkness, for the Scientific Leader returned sourly to his soup.

"And the buildings?" Jenny asked.

"Funny thing," Harkness said, smoothing the front of his crisp tunic. "You find some really cheap construction here, built during the Second Prosperity, where they used junk materials to reinforce the concrete. Oh, it worked well enough, for a while, but when the waters rose some of the metal was exposed to salt water and started to corrode. All the way through, sometimes, so you'll find a building with walls that look perfectly good, then you have the saser run on them and it turns out they're just loose concrete riddled with tunnels. About as safe and steady as a sand castle."

"Maybe less," Lonnie said, grinning. "Tobias always talks about all the good stuff he *could* have brought up from places like that."

"Good for fish, though," Li said. "How about it, Tobias? A couple of marlin ought to do us just fine, I could put one in stasis and, um, how about the other one in lime? Or white wine? With mushrooms, some garlic, red onions, tomatoes? What do you say?"

"Oh, for God's sake!" Tobias pushed himself away from the table. "What do you think I am, anyway? I didn't come aboard to do your shopping for you, you want fish you go down and get them yourself." He strode from the room and, after a slight hesitation, Jenny rose and followed him.

"Hey, you don't have to go, you know," Lonnie called to her. "He always throws a tantrum after dinner, it's good for his digestion. Let him sulk."

But Jenny shook her head and followed her lover from the room. Lonnie grinned, shrugged, and returned to her meal, but the conversation died.

28

Two years before Paul and Jenny came to the *Ilium* I was in Rome picking up a new valve set for my scuba equipment. Like every other location of any historical interest, Rome had been redone, refurbished, newly antiquated. Each hill was the possession of a particular epoch; each valley reflected a way of life dead for centuries, the interfaces between the replicated centuries sometimes sharp and clear, sometimes fading from one to the other in a confusion of times and styles. Tai-li's shop lay deep in the medieval sector; small cobble streets and alleys, houses and hovels packed densely together with little regard for what had actually occupied the area during the time being represented, picturesque and simulated squalor amid incongruous fountains and statues.

Rome is too cosmopolitan a city, however, to harbor those Immortals who dedicate themselves fiercely, for a decade or two, to living the day by day life of a past age. You have to travel to the Pyrenees to find villages where force-fields are strictly forbidden; you must delve deep into the African veldt to discover villages following cultures so old that even archaic zippers are under interdict. The Immortals playact with great enthusiasm at their living-games, and when they tire of them they move on, hopping casually from one century to another, exchanging cultures as easily as they exchange styles of clothing, and with as little knowledge of their composition. In Rome, however, the antiquity is merely a cover-up, and the force-furniture cleverly simulates wooden tables, stone benches, animal-skin rugs, and draperies. I was still building my house then, and sat in Tai-li's shop, sipping bitter coffee, contemplating the playacting of the Immortals with scorn.

Tai-li took the new valve set from a box and brushed it with her fingers.

"It's *almost* a completely true replication," she said. "I say almost because I didn't want to use the original materials, you understand. The rubber gives the air a vile taste. This is stabilized plasteen, a crystal, really. The set fits to the hose thus, then to the mask on this end, it should give you no problems. If it does, let me know."

"If it does I may not be in any position to let you know," I told her, and set down the pulsing cup.

"The other equipment's behaving itself?" she asked as she packed the set.

"Yes, the wet-suit works very well, stands up to use. You did a good job, Tai-li."

"I always do," she replied, and presented the payment plate. I pressed my thumb over the black surface. The signal pulsed and my purchase was complete. Tai-li ushered me to the door as we exchanged parting words and saw me out with relief. Tai-li valued my business; it gave her a legitimate reason to indulge her hobby of recreating the rubberized wonders of bygone days, but she didn't feel any more comfortable around me than did anyone else.

I stood for a moment in the hot summer sunlight, considering whether to stop for a cool drink before taking the tube back home. If I did stop, I would be stared at; well, let them stare. I wanted a drink and didn't mind clearing a cafe to get one.

I remembered seeing a cafe during the hop to Taili's shop, on the border of the large square that was the center of the twentieth-century restoration, and I began walking in that direction.

Heat danced and quivered over the street as I crossed from cobblestones to asphalt. Here the interface between centuries was abrupt; half-timbered, thatched buildings smack up against towering glass skyscrapers, each as fake as the other. I turned a corner and before me stretched the square, dotted with statues and fountains but not a tree in sight. It was surrounded on all sides by reconstructed twentieth-century buildings, all at least ten stories high, all hideously ugly, all seeming to move slightly as I stared at them through the heat waves. Hoppers scooted around the square, few people walked. I could see the cafe on the far side of the plaza, a pool of dark and welcoming shadow under awnings and umbrellas, and I started toward it.

A quarter of the way across the square, I was bathed in sweat and dizzy. I sat by a fountain, bereft of shade, and wet the sleeve of my suit, wiped my face, looked across what seemed an impossible distance toward the cafe. I should have called a hopper, I thought, but having embarked on my walk I would not turn back. I stood and began walking again, putting one foot before the other across the blistering flagstones. I stared at the sheets of rock under my feet, grey stone, white stone, brown stone, grey stone, brown stone, black lump.

Black lump?

The lump moved and I dropped to my knees. A cat, spread on the ground, panted slightly; an old cat, mangy, mangled by ancient battles fought under the whispered endlessness of slidebelts, or over the plastic thatched rooftops of a falsified past. I touched the cat,

but it ignored my hand and kept its eyes closed. Its
fur almost burned my fingers, and its head was tucked
around by its belly in a useless attempt to obtain some
shade. Old cat that had come into the square to die?
Old cat that hadn't come out to die, but was dying
anyway? I didn't doubt that the cat would not last
thirty minutes if left in the sunlight. I picked it up
carefully, pressed open the front seam of my suit and
thrust the cat inside, then began walking toward the
cafe again.

I reached another fountain, cupped a hand in the
water and offered it to the cat, who ignored it. Then I
dipped my finger in the water, forced it between its
teeth and managed to get some drops down the cat's
throat. No more response from the cat than before,
and only the slight movement of its belly against my
breasts told me that it lived. I splashed water on my
shirt, hoping it would cool both the cat and me, aligned
myself toward the still distant cafe, and began the trek
again.

Grey stone, brown stone, mottled stone, black stone,
brown stone, white stone, grey stone; how many
stones are there in the universe? How many stones in
that baked and sterile plaza? My feet were stones, my
neck, my head; the hair of my head was spun granite,
my arms marble, the cat lead. Old lead cat. Old lead
Tia. White stone grey stone brown stone white stone
and suddenly shade and voices; I looked from the
ground and found that I was within the cafe.

The voices died in concentric circles around me. I
sat heavily on a wooden chair, pulled the cat from my
suit, and laid it on the table before me.

"Bring me some water," I whispered to the waiter,
and a glass appeared promptly. I wetted a finger and
tried to pry open the cat's mouth. The jaw gave way
and hung slack, and I touched the wetness to the roof
of its mouth. The cat didn't move. I tried again.

"Please, thon, the cat is dead," the waiter said,
pained.

I trised to dribble some water down my finger into

the cat's mouth. The water ran over my fingernail, pooled in the red cavity and spilled out onto the table. The cat didn't move.

"Thon, please, the cat is dead," the waiter repeated, and took the glass from me. I looked up at him and back at the table.

The cat didn't move.

"Was it your cat, perhaps?"

"No, not my cat. No. Dead?"

"Sorry, yes. May I take it away?"

"Dead?"

"It's just an animal. Animals die, you know."

"Just animals."

"Of course." He handed me another glass of water and I sipped it, staring at the dead cat. It seemed to me, between one moment and the next, that it had begun to putrefy, that a stench filled the air, and I turned from it.

"Yes, take it away." The waiter summoned two others and together they gingerly slipped a floater under the entire table and guided it along the side of the cafe and out of sight.

"Would you care to order something?" the waiter asked when he returned. He centered a new table before me and, folding the floater neatly, slipped it into the pocket of his pants.

"Just, no. Nothing. What are you going to do with the cat?"

"It's been fed down the disposal system, of course."

"Of course."

"It was just an animal. Had to die sooner or later."

"Then what about me?" I demanded. He looked startled, straightened.

"Yes, thon?" Politely. Fake innocence. Staring at my face.

"Yes, me, Tia Grasshopper. Am I an animal?"

"No, thon, not at all."

"Wrong. We're all animals, we just forget it whenever we can, is all." I might as well have spoken gibberish, for all the understanding in his green eyes.

"Get me a hopper, please. Right now."

"Yes, thon," he said with relief, and very soon one waited before the cafe, gate open. I stood, walked through the silent people, entered the hopper, and the gate closed firmly.

I punched the buttons for the tube station and sat back, weary, as the hopper hummed, picked up speed, and rushed away from the barren square.

ᘓ 29 ᘔ

Pretty Paul lies in my hammock, foot idly swinging back and forth, and he puffs upon a joint.

"Off," I say to him. "I want to wash the blanket, remove yourself."

And he has a tantrum. He does not want the blanket gone, he does not want to rise, he does not want to go to his room, he does not want to lie on the hammock's cords, he wants nothing but to recline in blissful idleness. I insist, he resists, and within five minutes an argument is in full flower. Eventually, in the heat of battle, he quits the hammock to harangue me at closer range, and I neatly lift the blanket from the bed, toss it in the vibra, and punch the button. Paul hits me. I hit him back.

Ten minutes later he is contrite, apologetic, cringing, flattering. I am disgusted, angry, impolite, and abusive, but let him back in anyway. Don't ask me why.

"No," says Harkness with sarcastic patience. "If we

go down here, where you want, we'll be a league south of Hilo, and will have to maneuver underwater. Hilo is *here*." And he stabs a finger at the map.

"I'm not so sure about that," Greville says pompously. "If we go down where I want to, we'll have a better view of what we're after. . . ."

"Nonsense. Visibility underwater is lousy," and Harkness reaches around the Scientific Leader to punch his own directions into the computer. Greville, controlling himself, announces that in his considered opinion a grave error has been made, for which he cannot, in fairness, accept any blame whatsoever. Harkness maintains a contemptuous silence; Greville stalks to the door, but before he reaches it his control breaks and he stomps out, goes down to his cabin where he will spend the next hour breaking tiny sticks of wood into many pieces and writing drafts of resignation. Up in the bridge, Harkness and Hart giggle together. Greville doesn't miss dinner.

Beautiful Tobias burns. Angered or insulted, he smoulders about the ship, broadcasting darkness as he goes. Anger fit for cataclysmic occurrences, fit for catastrophic dooms.

I come down a corridor, my arms loaded with bits and pieces of my back-up suit, to meet Tobias coming up from the hold with a gauge in his hand. I begin to sidestep, but he leans toward me, blocks me, and his eyes are hot.

"Ti-a," he said, turning my name into two distinct syllables. "Do you have any children, Ti-a?"

"Go away," I mutter, try to move around him.

"Any children? Any little children?"

"What do you think?" I say, angrily, and push him aside. His whisper follows me down the corridor, "children, children, children," until I plunge down a droptube, stuff my equipment in my locker, and flee to my minaret. I will give him credit for this, though: I do not think he knows how much his question hurts.

Another time I raise my head from an exhibit in the

ship's museum to find Tobias behind me. As I turn, he whispers, "I'm twenty-three, Ti-a. I'm twenty-three," before he kicks his floater and rushes down the arcade and away. I shrug and turn toward the exhibit again. This is Tobias, playing at the very edge, gilding the emotional dandelion. Why? Does Jenny know of this? It makes no difference, really. Tobias burns.

Jenny, angered, spins in chaos, searching for rationality. She pursues the elusive cause and loses her fury in misunderstanding, in an often useless quest for comprehension and sense. Jenny's pain is misinterpreted and she destroys her searching by a refusal to accept the obvious. Or so I think. Lonnie thinks her nosy, Benito thinks her silly, Paul thinks her stupid.

Despite the sunlight, she seems more pale than she did a week ago at the edge of the sea. She seems more nervous, she seems lost. The glances that she gives Paul are no longer those of hate, but those of confusion, almost of understanding and pity. But she is still uncomfortable with me, despite our sunlit, minaret talk. I'm not sure I understand Jenny, I'm almost sure that I like her. But beauty does not reside with beast.

In a midnight wandering I pass Li's cabin and hear the sounds of music. Unwilling to eavesdrop, I nonetheless hear our fat and fatuous cook singing to the accompaniment of some stringed instrument, and what he sings is soft and simple and infinitely sad. I am drawn to it, knock softly upon the cabin door. Li puts down the instrument. Lonnie and Hart look up with surprise, and all make nervous, giggling comments. I leave them, and soon the soft plunking of the instrument sounds again.

And Benito, locked away from me, I do not see at all.

30

"Paul?"

He wasn't in the diving hold, where he should have been, or in the museum, where he often was. I glanced down the brightly-lit hall again, hands on hips, and turned my back on the displays. We were coming into position over the island, and I had asked Paul to be in the diving hold for a last dry run of his equipment and the ship's diving regulations before the first dive next morning. I hadn't expected him to be on time, that would have been asking too much, but I had expected him to show up sooner or later. An hour had gone by before I had exhausted my patience and gone looking for him. And now I couldn't find him.

I dropped to the galley and peered into the room on the chance that Paul might have decided to raid Li's pantry rather than request a less appetizing snack from the ship's console system. Li stood by one of the workfields, fine white flour streaked down the front of his dark-blue worksuit, while fruit tarts shaped themselves under his swift fingers.

"Seen Paul?" I asked.

"What? No, not since mess."

"Okay, thanks."

"Hey, Tia, you think Tobias will bring me a fish after all?"

"I don't know, Li. Would you like me to bring you one?"

"Uh, no thanks. I can manage." Li looked embarrassed. "I just like to tease him, you know?"

"Yeah, I know," I said, leaving the galley. I would have been more than happy to spear a marlin for Li, but he always refused my offers. Occasionally I believed that his superstitions must include something about the communicability of mortality, but considered the idea with more amusement than anything else. Li wasn't an important part of my life.

I bounced to the bridge and glanced in quickly. Deserted, the banks happily blinking and bleeping to themselves. Harkness wouldn't feel the need to play captain until we actually maneuvered into position, in about four hours' time. Our fearless captain would, as usual, spend the interim enthusiastically buggering Hart in his cabin, dissipating tensions and clearing his mind for the complicated, tricky job before him, a job the computer could have done just as well, and with less circumstance. In the meantime, no Hart, no Harkness, and no Paul either. My exasperation slowly moved toward anger.

My cabin? More likely than his. He seemed to enjoy spending time in my hammock, lying back with his eyes focussed on nothing or, more rarely, glancing through one of my dense and archaic paper-bound books.

I dropped from the bridge to third level, grabbed a floater, and kicked it down the patterned hallway.

Third level centered about a deep well that rose from second level toward the sky and was protected at the top by a Victorian glass-work cage which admitted light and fresh air, but was itself protected by an invisible force-field. Most third level cabins opened onto the filigreed balcony circling the well, but I had chosen one that opened onto a small side corridor; three ports in my cabin looked off the starboard side of the *Ilium,* and the corridor opening granted me greater privacy than the more public openings to the balcony cabins.

I flicked the floater across the emptiness of the well, maneuvered down my corridor, and palmed open the door, all in one easy movement.

They froze as I entered. Lonnie was perched precariously above Paul in the hammock, and both looked at me with expressions of complete amazement. I, equally amazed, stood speechless, and the automatic masks of self-defense clamped over my emotions before I even thought of shock or pain. I dug my fists into my hips and glowered.

"Uh, hi," Lonnie offered. "Paul said you were busy."

"In the diving hold," he added.

"Indeed. Perhaps you forgot that you were supposed to be there, too?" Paul looked blank. "Listen, we're diving tomorrow, or don't you remember? I want one last dry run with you before we go down, because you need one. I don't intend to clear you with Greville until I'm completely sure you can handle the dive. I'll be in the hold for another hour. You want to dive, you'll be there."

I stepped out of the room and slapped the door shut. Gunning the floater viciously, I whipped around the corner onto the balcony, across the well and down the droptubes to the hold, where I kicked the floater toward a corner and paced. I had barely managed to control the shaking of my body before Paul dropped to the hold.

"Get your equipment out," I commanded. "Identify each piece as to name and function, set them in order and check them."

He did so silently, placing the various parts of the bubble-suit in a line on the floor, then stood and waited for me to check them over. I glanced at them quickly.

"Get on with it."

He identified each one as he lifted it for an inspection, his tone subdued. I corrected his mistakes, took him through the inspection again, created some hypothetical emergencies that he coped with acceptably, and told him to stow the equipment. I turned to go before he had finished, but he sprinted after me, grabbed my shoulder, and pulled me around to him.

"Don't paw me!" I cried, jerking away from his hands. "Leave me alone!"

"Tia, please, I wouldn't have done it if I thought you were going to be so upset. . . ."

"I don't care! You were supposed to be here for the run, you can at least observe your own schedules."

"I'm sorry, really I am, Tia. After all, you know, it's *you* I love."

"We're not talking about that. I don't give a damn what you do with your spare time, but when we've made arrangements to do something connected with the dive, I damn well expect you to be here, not off, off. . . ." And, to my dismay, I felt my nose stuff up and redden, my eyes prickle with tears.

"Tia, please don't cry," Paul begged. I barely comprehended his agitation through my misery.

"And besides, you didn't have to do it on my hammock."

"But Lonnie hadn't ever done it in a hammock," he said. "She was curious, that's all."

"Then you could have gotten your own hammock."

"Aw, Tia, don't be that way. You didn't used to be selfish about your stuff."

"I was, that was a whole 'nother woman, don't you see? I'm not the same as her, she could afford to spread it around, she wasn't going to lose it all." And this time I did break down, sobbing into my hands and angrily refusing Paul's confused gestures of comfort. It was an amorphous sort of weeping, compounded in part of more than a little self-pity, some anger at Paul and Lonnie and more at myself, and a strong sense of be-

trayal that, as soon as I found it, stopped the sobs. I
didn't own him. I hadn't been so stupid as to believe
that an archaic sense of fidelity had anything to do
with this affair, had I? The return of my sense of idiocy brought with it a return of rationality, and I
mopped my face with my sleeve, blew my nose, and
generally composed myself. Paul looked infinitely relieved by my recovery.

"Look, Tia. . . ."

"No, just be quiet. Put the stuff away, okay?"

"Sure. You'll be in to lunch?"

I shrugged and left the hold before he could venture
any further comments.

The rainbow, on examination, had faded even further. I didn't even like Paul very much, I decided, but
the thought of barring him from my cabin was still
painful. I soothed myself with adages: Beggars can't
be choosers, gift horses and mouths, and, finally, one
of my own creations: Pride has nothing to do with it.

I battered the subject about until I grew thoroughly
sick of it, then went down to lunch.

31

I pulled the legs of my wet-suit over my thighs, shifting and urging the thick, balky rubber into place. I had finished helping Paul into his bubble-suit and Tobias was putting the finishing touches on Jenny's suit before readying himself. Lonnie, the list in her hand, was checking Paul's equipment, her murmured words the only sound in the otherwise silent hold. Tobias finished with Jenny; she walked down the rough-surfaced ramp to the lower level and sat at the edge of the diving well. I wriggled into the top of my suit, checking seams and fastenings, closed the seals, settled the tanks and jets on my back. I pulled the black rubber headsheath over my hair and Tobias appeared behind me, set the seams on the sheath and checked for unwanted apertures. When he had finished I closed the connections on the back of his waistband, securing each shunt to its proper place. Safety took precedence over our mutual dislike, and we checked each other's rigs before diving with a maximum of skill and a minimum of civility. He moved away. I scooped up my flippers and took my place by the diving well. Tobias sat a moment later, waiting for Lonnie to begin his check, while Greville from the bridge observed us all on the vidsystem. The tension in the air almost sang.

The three Immortals were each encased in the network of dark blue and red wires and golden electrodes that comprised the bubble mechanisms; the vermilion bundle of equipment lay beside each one on the smooth, multi-colored floor. Their tanned bodies, firm and smooth, glowed through the crossings of wire, the bandings of fabric; beside them I looked even more the troglodite, encased in black rubber. The tanks on my back mocked Benito's hump, hoses trailed over my shoulders, waist loaded with metal weights and pieces of equipment. Jenny stared at me from the corner of her eye and I resisted the impulse to snap shut the clear shield of my faceplate.

Twenty minutes crawled by before Tobias and I were finally checked out, then the intercom coughed.

"Friends, you are now ready to dive," Greville announced from the bridge. "You have all been briefed on safety precautions, so I won't go into that again. Yes. Ahem. Tobias will dive first, then Paul, then Jenny, and Tia will take up the rear. The remotes are already waiting for you below the surface. Ahem. Do be careful. Okay."

Tobias dropped first, the field forming around him as he slid into the water below the lip of the well. He held position for a moment while the field finished forming over his head, then slipped down and to the side, motioning Paul to follow. I activated my radio so that I could hear them.

"Slowly," Tobias was saying. "Feet first and, wait a minute, okay, now touch the activating lever. *Slowly*. Fine. Keep coming. Stop now, let it finish. Right. Now come all the way under. Take your time. Good."

Paul glanced up at me, smiling, through layers of force and layers of water. I nodded at him, then Jenny

coolly slid into the water as though she had done it innumerable times before. When the three Immortals
were clear of the well, I snapped my face-plate shut,
activated the tanks and tumbled over the side into the
cool ocean.

The ocean made space for me, pressing against the
blackness of my assumed skin, buoying me and
counter-acting the heaviness of the lead fastened
around my waist. I kicked and continued my initial
dive, feeling the pressures sliding back against my belly
and legs, the quiet acceptance of the seas. Space and
ocean have much in common, both are alien to us, not
our element, both contain mysteries, dangers, sudden
beauties of their own and beyond our land-bound experience. But space is a container of nothingness, a
vacuum, a void of immeasurable loneliness and occasional transcendence. Water is a repository of life,
and the life asserts itself as you move through the
ocean; creatures large and small, beautiful or stun-
ningly grotesque according to their custom, aquatic
forests and microscopic landscapes, beings caught between the layers of life, rocks made of living creatures
and living creatures made of stone, vegetable animals
and animated plants and sudden deep, heart-breaking,
lovely jewels that flick their trailing rainbows and dart
away from you between the fronds of weeds, leaving
shimmering mysteries that can be pursued, but never
truly caught and comprehended.

Space does not care whether you are there or not,
and the struggle to survive between worlds is a fight
to avoid being sucked into vacuum, into an ultimate
nil. Implacable in its indifference, it kills you simply
because it *is,* and crushes you with the weight of your
knowledge of its indifference. But the ocean is not
indifferent. It reacts and shapes itself to your presence
or absence, presents its laws as implacable realities, but
an instant later displays the very non-exemplar of that
rule swimming calmly through the depths. Accept the
strangeness and the ocean opens to you, gives you
freedom and beauty, a hook into otherness. But wonder

approached in fear is cancelled, disappears into threatening shiverings of distant plants, into terrifying movements of bulky darkness through the rocks.

Here, near the surface, the world of water shimmered with light and color. I caught Jenny's eye and gestured upward, and she raised her head to see the mantle of the shining sea. Paul stared morosely down into the darkness.

We moved slowly through the first atmosphere, and the remotes followed like faithful sentries. I thumbed on my jets and closed the gap between Jenny's bubble and myself. She floated lightly in the center of her sphere of air, her head constantly moving as she tried to see 360° around her simultaneously. Ahead of her, Paul started when a large marlin swam by superciliously, and only relaxed once the large fish was out of sight. By moving to one side, I could see Tobias already peering down at the ruins below us. Two of the remotes streaked away in response to his signal.

"Do you have visual contact yet?" Greville demanded in his best scientific voice.

"Yes, looks like a hotel," Tobias reported as we approached the buildings. "There're some lower spots that look like they were swimming pools, and lots of windows. All broken. Lots of silt. Maybe ten, twelve levels originally, the first one's double size."

The remotes had reached the first building. I detached the small screen from my belt and held it before my face-plate. "It appears to be a lobby," Tobias continued. "Have you got the picture?"

"Yes, resolution's fine," Greville replied. "Can you implement holo-projection?"

"Not yet," I said. "Wait until we get there ourselves."

Sudden light spilled from the building below; the second remote had entered and set up the floods. I keyed its transmission to my screen and Tobias had it begin a slow pan of the lobby.

"Tune second," I told Greville. "There's the desk, elevator banks, couple of doors, some steps leading out toward the back of the building. Everything's pretty much a shambles."

"What are the stress factors?" Greville snapped.

"Wait until I get a reading," I replied, amused and a bit impatient. Greville always took the opportunity of a dive to be as scientific and "in command" as he could possibly be, and more often than not his attempts to be professional only got in the way. I set one of the remotes to probing the walls, and the saser beams bounced back to create a three-dimensional color image on my screen. Red lines for the steel beams, blue haze for concrete, bright yellow stress patterns of molecules under pressure. The remote tracked along the wall while I studied the image on my screen, ignoring Greville's huffs of impatience.

"Yes, it's safe enough," I said finally. "Simple concrete and steel beam construction, some stress but not enough to worry about. Party wall construction inside, and the bearing wall integrity is good. The main lobby windows are big enough for the bubbles."

"Confirmed," Harkness' voice replied.

"Good," said Greville. "Post remotes and enter at will."

We reached the building and one of the remotes stationed itself by a window to relay our communications to the ship, while four others removed the remaining shards of broken glass from the window and entered, turning on their lights as they took up positions in the four corners of the large room. The image on my belt screen showed the lights of their holocameras flickering to life, and suddenly the image was multidimensional.

Tobias held us up for a moment while he made a show of searching the window frames for broken glass, then slipped into the lobby. Paul followed, bouncing once from the side of the window when he underestimated his clearance. Jenny went through with little trouble and I swam in behind her.

"Has entrance been effected?" Greville inquired.

"Yes, everything's clear."

"Good. Find the main office," Greville directed. "These places usually had a safe."

And the looting was on.

Antiquities. Glass jewelry mocking the finest gems, wristwatches, vases, sculpture, paintings, anything, everything. Greville's home was already stuffed with things taken from the houses of the dead; Tobias' fine collection traveled with him aboard the *Ilium*. Each of the other crew except, perhaps, Benito, had a cache of treasures. Stuffed sportfish. Stainless from the kitchens. Ersatz flowers. China. Stemware. Plastic coats. Devices for curling hair. Porcelain faucets from the bathrooms—these were especially popular, more so when they came from resort hotels and were shaped like women or fish. Old plastic currency. Electric toothcleaners. Mirrors. Archaic vid-phones. Liquid crystal clocks, long defunct. Rubber boots. Telecommunications equipment. Plasticized greeting cards. Spectacles. True, some of the stuff found its way into museums, some into the *Ilium*'s collection, but most was either sold to collectors or vanished into the crew's private accumulations. Never mind what it was once for, or why it was created, or when it was used. Never mind what the lives of its original owners were like. It doesn't matter what it ultimately means, what it says about the culture that created and used it. It's a curiosity, a gimcrack, a decoration, a pretty, and no other meaning is necessary. Jenny and Paul would leave the *Ilium* with their separate piles of treasure, each lovingly hand-stolen from the bottom of the sea.

I left the Immortals to their scavenging and busied myself correcting the angles of the holo-cameras. I had just finished when Tobias announced that they had cracked the safe, and I swam over to see.

It was a large safe, set into the side of the main office. The walls of the room were cracking and peeling around it, but the strong metal sides of the safe were intact, uncompromisingly rectangular amid the dissolving planes and angles of the room. The Great

Shaping had delivered enough of a jolt to the room to twist the heavy door on its hinges, and water had entered the safe. Paul and Jenny hovered to one side, the utility remote retracted its implements while a second remote wrenched the door from its hinges and laid it on the floor. I raised my belt screen as the first remote entered the safe and began broadcasting.

"It's hard to tell," Tobias said. "Boxes, some stuff on the shelves, a few things on the floor. There couldn't have been much in here when the place went down."

"Well, check it over," Greville demanded, dropping all pretense of scientific detachment. "There's got to be *something* of value."

The remotes began hauling stuff from the safe and loading it onto a field web. There was nothing of any interest to me, and I left the room.

"Greville, I'm going to take a look at some of the other buildings," I said into my radio.

"Take a remote," he said automatically, unnecessarily. I didn't bother to reply, but when I left the hotel I signaled one of the outside remotes to tag along, and kicked myself upward until I could see over the lower wing of the building.

At ten meters down, all colors but blues and greys were washed from the spectrum, and I floated in a subdued and eerie world, a universe the color of liquid ashes and suspended dust. The Immortals, of course, turned on their lights as soon as they dropped through the first atmosphere, restoring reds, oranges, yellows to the spectrum, and the further down they dove, the less they saw outside their cone of illumination. Peering from the window of the hotel before I swam from it, it had seemed that I was leaving a world of light for a world of darkness, but the illusion melted as soon as I was far enough from the lights so that the natural illumination of the ocean was restored. I squinted through the somber sea, made out a bulk which, on closer inspection, turned out to be a second hotel in a great state of disrepair. I angled away from it and two strong kicks sufficed to send me gliding, jetless, toward the submerged hump of the island's saddle-back. I rose slowly, keeping the bed of the ocean a meter below me, pacing the rise of the land. A cracked roadbed lay below me, indicated only by the slight flat valley it made between the ruined hulks and humps of buildings. Seaplants waved, small fish darted through the waters, and the silence was profound, endless, complete. I glided through it, a small speck trailing through the calm waters, trailed itself by the smaller speck that was the remote.

As I rose, the blues and greys became tinged with green, then with yellow as I came into the first atmosphere. I had been carefully inspecting each building that I passed, but most were too ruined to be either safe or interesting. Then, toward the mountain-side, I saw what looked to be an almost perfectly preserved building, nestled in a small depression in the hill. I flicked my jets open, glanced behind to see that the remote followed, and streaked toward it.

"Hey, look at this one," Paul's voice said, and I glanced at my screen. The three Immortals clustered around one of the remotes, which held in its pick-up arm the broken piece of a chandelier.

"It's a sculpture," Tobias said importantly. "The Ancients worked with glass a lot during the second or third century before the Shaping. This one's probably valuable."

"Careful with it," Greville directed. "Be careful."

The remote continued holding the collection of prisms while the three admired it. The strong, clear light cancelled the reflections of their bubble-suits, so that they looked as though they were floating unprotected in the deeps, the blue and red of their veins somehow misplaced and lying in intricate lace patterns over the gold of their skins. Behind them, moss and seaplants waved gently over the walls of the room, while below them lay gleaming piles of booty. Some small glittering fish swam into the room, moved through the plants, then bolted as the remote placed the chandelier atop the rest of the loot. Tobias, Paul and Jenny, oblivious to the fish, were already staring greedily into the mouth of the safe.

I replaced the screen, turned down the volume on the radio, and continued toward the small building.

32

The building had no windows at all. I circled it twice, flooded the walls with light, and peered at the crumbling plaster and the thick solid-looking blocks of stone beneath. One entrance, centered in one of the short walls of the rectangle, was covered by waving seaplants, hesitant mosses. The hinges of the door had rotted away, and the thick plank hung askew over the opening. I lay my hand against the stones, puzzled; anything that solid, of that construction, would have lacked the resiliency necessary to move with and survive the Great Shaping, should have tumbled under the shocks and cracked under the sinking. I had the remote probe the walls, and watched while the image formed on my screen; the red streaks of steel beams and cable, not in the usual up and down, side to side construction pattern, but webbed, interlocked, creating innumerable polygons running the length and width of the wall, and more than allowing for the resiliency the building had to possess. The stones, according to the saser probe, were nothing more than deep lines carved into the sides of the building to simulate rock. I "peeled" the outer layer of image from the screen and found that the webbed wall construction ran through the entire structure. There were no party walls at all. A solid construction, almost a monument, built to last. Why?

No windows, no ventilation shafts, one door. No carvings over the doorway, no indication of function. A tomb? No, not in twenty-first century Hilo. A monument, then? For what purpose? And what self-respecting monument lacked an inscription? The probe indicated two levels of rooms within—hallways, doors, ceilings, floors. Functional, obviously, but functional for what?

Mystery, mystery. I hovered before the opening and felt excitement flaring through me. The seaplants danced with the motion of small fish, the darkness seemed to flow outward, beckoning. I restrained myself from plunging headlong into the terrifying, welcoming mouth of the building and signalled the remote to activate its lights and enter.

"Tia, what have you found?" Greville's voice demanded, a small, insistent whine at my ear. The rape of the main safe was probably completed, and he had found a moment to remember me while the other divers searched for more plunder. I sighed and turned up the radio.

"It's hard to tell," I replied. "It's a building, but I can't figure out its function. Certainly not residential. Solid, no obvious damage, no windows, the door's open. About fifteen meters high, same width and length. I want to go in."

"Now, Tia, it might be unduly dangerous," Greville's prissy voice advised. "Wait until we get some more remotes to you, all right?"

"Why? I've got one remote already, and the probe shows surprisingly little stress."

"At least wait until Tobias and the others finish

with the hotel and get to you, they'll be able to go in
with you."

"No, they won't fit through the entrance. Perish,
Greville, just let me get on with it, will you?"

"At least leave a remote out to relay!"

"All right, all right," I muttered, and glanced down
at my beltscreen before signalling the remote. The
screen showed no picture at all.

I propelled myself to the door and grabbed the
frame. As soon as I entered, I saw the remote before
me and my screen leaped to life, still set to saser. I
switched to visual pick-up and the red webs disappeared, became a simple, concrete view of the flooded
and darkened lobby. I moved outside again and the
image on my screen faded, disappeared.

"Greville, the walls seem to block everything except
line-of-sight transmission," I said. "I'll have to leave
LOS transmitters as I go, so talk-back will be a bit
fuzzy."

I dove back into the building before he had a
chance to object, and took my time signalling the
remote to take its station before the door. Then,
activating my lights and loosening my stunner in its
sheath, I moved deeper into the building.

The remains of chairs and sofas rotted along the
walls, the fabric and cushions replaced by shivering
plants. A metal desk at the far end of the room, moss-
covered and rusting, bore complex, archaic communications equipment, the skeletons of writing implements,
and a residue of paper in the one drawer I was able to
open. Small tables, corroded lamps, disintegrated reading matter. No inscriptions, nothing indicating the purpose of the building.

Directly to the right of the desk a door hung on one
hinge. I pushed it and it floated to the floor, its descent
terrifying a school of small, skittering fish. I took my
main light bank from the desk and entered the next
room, a large hall with many doors opening from it
and metal chairs positioned neatly about the walls.
One large stairwell led upward from the room, and

beside it rested the closed doors of an elevator. Seaplants, amid the detritus on the floors and chairs, bent
and swayed in the wake of my passing, and small
creatures scuttled about the legs of the furniture as I
moved through the rooms surrounding the main waiting area. Each door had a number engraved upon it,
some illegible and none completely intact; it took me a
moment to realize that none of the numbers were in
sequence, and I could not find a pattern governing
their arrangement. The doors quaked and fell as I
touched them, raising clouds of silt that billowed
through the water and sank slowly again, reflecting the
brilliance of my lights in pointillist shimmers against
the darker waters. Desks, chairs, filing cabinets, communications terminals, computer terminals, writing
machines, talking machines, one room lined with hard-
bound books whose rotting covers shook and ran down
my hands as I lifted them. No clues. I opened the last
door at the far end of the room and a large, glutinous
creature darted from the darkness and as quickly retreated. Another hall, here, with rooms branching out
—each contained high tables and rotting machinery,
small instruments, occasional locked cases with glass
doors that were clear sheets of silver in the light. The
furthest door opened into what was obviously a ward;
the beds were lined up in a double row, each parallel to
the other, each now the silted bed of sealife. A clinic,
then? A hospital? But for some reason it simply did not
feel like a medical place, and I had been in enough of
them to trust my instincts. I swam back slowly to the
waiting room and contemplated the stairs. I was about
to ascend them when I remembered the LOS transmitters. I returned to the lobby and began planting the
small objects along the walls, through the waiting room,
up the stairs. I waited until I had the last of them in
place at the top of the stairwell before boosting the
volume on my receiver.

". . . where the hell are you?" Greville shrieked.
"Tia, will you answer me?"

"I'm still in the building," I said calmly.

"Oh! We can't pick up your homer, and you weren't transmitting," he complained.

"Sorry, I forgot about the transmitters. They're up now."

"You forgot! You forgot! How could you forget something like that?"

"Sorry, I was involved in what I was doing."

"Anything of interest?"

"No," I lied easily. "I'll let you know."

I turned down the volume and continued up to the hallway, slapping transmitters against the walls as I went.

This corridor ran the breadth of the building, from one wall to another. Again the multitude of doors, but here were no neatly placed chairs, no small tables bearing the remains of lamps. I swam to my right, down to the very end of the hall, and made my way back toward the stairwell, entering each room in turn. The first one, nearest the outer wall, held high tables and laboratory equipment. One wall was lined with metal cages in which grew small microcosms, tiny gardens of plants and animals, beautiful and strange. Lying amid the seagardens were small, pale bones, probably those of mammals trapped in their cages when the island sank. Monolithic cases of machinery lined a second wall. Each hulking unit was replete with dials and knobs, screens and nodes. Again no clues, and the building still didn't feel like a hospital to me. More rooms, more offices, another liquid library, a closet containing the remains of ancient cleaning equipment, a room with four beds and a large mirror, a room beside that one holding a desk, chair, and the backside of the mirror; a window looking into the small ward. The stairwell, more offices, a few rooms whose functions I could not immediately determine. A file room. The last room on the right, equally as large as its counterpart at the far end of the hall, held a large cylindrical tank and some rotting apparatus suspended above it. Banks of equipment lined its outer sides and bulged with gauges, dials, screens, knobs, sockets. Directly beside this room was one with a single bed and what seemed to be primitive monitoring equipment along a wall, one chair, and a cabinet of bottles and instruments covered with moss. Another large room on the left side of the corridor, with the remains of furniture and pillows, an old sound-reproduction machine, many frames hanging on the walls, but the pictures within the frames were gone, eaten by the sea. A screen.

I returned to the hall and floated motionless, trying to make sense of the building and its contents. A research facility? Possibly, but what goal was being pursued? A clinic? Doubtful, but only because that definite hospital sense was nowhere in evidence. I could have been mistaken, and yet, and yet . . .

I turned up my radio and listened in on the doings of my fellow divers. They seemed to have made their way up to the hotel rooms and were busy removing bulbs from sockets, wrenching faucets from bathroom equipment, yanking hangers from closets, taking various small trays and other objects. Greville wouldn't miss my remote for some time, so I signalled it to slap a general transmitter on the outer wall of the building and come to me. I wanted desperately to make sense of the building, and another saser probe seemed to be the only thing I could manage. Maybe the image would be different from the second floor, maybe a probe would discover something on which I could hang a theory, maybe I was just wasting my time creating and pursuing mysteries where none existed, maybe the building was simply a madman's folly and nothing more. Still, the solid construction, the blocking of transmissions, the incomprehensible rooms. . . .

The probe revealed the same pattern as before, both on walls and on floors. Then, impulsively, I directed the beams toward the ceiling, and discovered a third level.

But there were no stairwells leading beyond the

second level. I searched, and when I failed to find one I had the remote pry open the elevator doors and I swam up the shaft. Cables, winches, smooth sides, but no openings. I tapped on the walls with the butt of my stunner, and instead of receiving the sound of solidity or the sound of water-filled space, the echo that bounced back to me meant only one thing—air trapped under the layers of the ocean.

My heart was racing. I held to the elevator cable and breathed deeply until the blood moved more decorously through my veins, then returned to the corridor and examined the ceiling, tuning the remote to medium magnification and studying the images on my screen. At the very end of the corridor I found a faint, square indentation amid the moss and discolorations above my head.

The remote built a seal around the entrance, a transparent wall of force extending from the ceiling to the floor and encompassing it and myself. When it was finished I had air pumped into the seal from the remote's store. The full force of gravity grabbed me as the water emptied from the bubble, and I cursed quietly as I realized that the square was now a good meter above my head. Well, there was no help for it; I removed my flippers and weights, clambered atop the remote and pushed at the square. It didn't budge. I activated my vibra-knife and sliced around its edges, then shoved against the hatch again. It resisted for a moment, then moved heavily, and I pushed it up and away from the opening. A rush of air blew upward past my face, and below me the remote released more oxygen from its tanks. I checked my balance, then jumped, grasped the edge of the opening and pulled myself upward, twisted and sat at the edge of the square hole. The remote scooped up my discarded equipment and, extending one arm to hook over the edge of the hole, pulled itself up into the darkness with me. I felt a slight shifting along my skin as the seal enlarged to encompass the entire room, then the

remote's lights flashed on and the room leaped into
dimension around me.

A low archway divided the small area in which I
sat from the main room and, lying along the curve of
the arch, were the words MITSUYAGA FECIT, PRO
BONO HOMINIS.

What the hell?

⊰ 33 ⊱

MITSUYAGA, GEORGE ANDREAS. Born
2005 A.D., Molokai, Hawaii. Married: Mitsuko
Hayakawa, 2025, div. 2027. Married: Jean An-
derssen, 2030, div. 2055. No children. President:
Hilo National Bank; Pacific Shipping & Steamship
Co., Ltd.; East-West Imports, Inc.; International
Electronics; Psychic Research Center of Hilo;
Apollo Industries. Chairman of Board: American
Amalgamated, Inc.; Far East Transport Co.; In-
dustrias Mexicanas, S.A.; International Telecom-
munications Systems, Inc.; Hanover Studies
Institute. Author: THE INNER LIGHT; STUD-
IES IN PARAPSYCHOLOGY; A HISTORY
OF PSYCHIC PHENOMENA; MIND OVER
MATTER; THE ULTIMATE STEP. Leading
proponent of theory of immortality through psy-
chic control, founder of Teleability Screening &
Research Centers. Philanthropist. Committed

2087 Hilo Institute for the Gifted Insane. Died
2094, Hilo, Hawaii.

From BRIEF WHO'S WHO OF THE MINDS OF
AMERICA, published 2102 Pre-Shaping, Alfred
Greengarten & Co., New York, New York, U.S.A.
Preserved in the Library at Luna.

It doesn't tell the half of it.

34

So I stood and entered the room, pausing, hesitating, staring at the convoluted, cryptic objects that appeared in the light of my beams. The ceiling, walls, floor, were all flocked with some soft, black material that rounded the edges and gave the room a feeling of depth, a womb-feeling. I peeled one glove from my hand and touched the wall; it was cold and gave slightly below my palm. Various humps and irregularities took form as I moved past them, revealing themselves as machines, monitors, somethings lying solemn and dead in my path. I made a complete circuit of the room, then returned to the hatch and looked back into the darkness, wondering.

The remote's clear-air signal winked on, and I flicked the valves of my equipment shut, removed my tanks and mask and piled them neatly on the floor; their rubbery black contrasted oddly with the deeper richness of the surface on which they rested. I touched

them, felt their reassuring solidity, then ran my uncovered hands over the archway. It was flocked also,
but with a silvery material, and the letters above had
been lifted into relief by thicknesses of grey. Mitsuyaga? And the rest, Latin? Fecit, facilitate, factory,
factotum—to make? Made, then. Mitsuyaga made,
what? This? Pro, propound, promote, protect? Produce? Mitsuyaga made (?) bono, bonus, benefactor
—bene, good? Hominis, easy, humanity. Mitsuyaga
made, good of humanity. Mitsuyaga made this for the
good of humanity. Okay. Who in hell was Mitsuyaga?

I found another silvery spot embedded in the black
along the thickness of the archway. I touched it and
it gave beneath my fingers, a definite "click" but nothing happened. Ah, current, electricity, something to
run the sulking machines. A generator, then, somewhere in the building? Or depending on outside
sources, tied in with the city's lines? I probed the spot,
feeling, prying, and eventually the cover yielded to
my prodding, slipped out to lay in my palm. Wiring
beneath, archaic. I had seen representations of pre-
Shaping wiring in diagrams, in books, among Benito's
collection of mechanical oddities, but I had never
needed to work with it myself. I paused, stared,
thought. Ground? This one, probably, and this one
hot. Would I get away with introducing current into
the system from this point?

I shrugged suddenly and beckoned the remote, had
it send pulses through each of the wires, watching the
diagrams appear as clean white lines over the blackness of my screen. Seemed simple enough. I matched
currents and programmed the machine to feed electricity into the wiring and, after a few false starts, the
room vibrated with an almost subliminal humming;
the wall on which I leaned grew warm beneath me.

A gentle light washed through the room, was absorbed into the soft black surfaces. I approached the
first protruding hulk by the door and soon found another silvery spot. Hesitation, then determination; I
pushed the spot and stood back quickly, concentrating

on the machine, poised for flight. A humming of a
different pitch, the side of the machine exchanged
blackness for translucency and a series of still, hologrammatic images rolled before me.

The first one said:

ENGLISH	TAGALOG	SWAHILI
FRENCH	CHINESE	HEBREW
GERMAN	JAPANESE	TURKISH
ITALIAN	BURMESE	GREEK
SPANISH	HINDI	CELTIC
DANISH	URDU	ARABIC
	OTHER	

I stared at it. A list of languages, but whatever for?
The picture waited and I waited, and finally I said
"English" aloud. Nothing. So I touched the screen beside the word and jerked my hand back as the picture
dissolved into blackness. Brief pause, and words
reeled across the screen:

WELCOME. IF THESE WORDS ARE PASSING
TOO QUICKLY FOR YOUR COMPREHENSION,
YOU MAY TOUCH THE SCREEN AND THE IM-
AGE WILL FREEZE UNTIL THE SCREEN IS
TOUCHED AGAIN. PLEASE SIT DOWN. THE
FLOOR WILL DO NICELY. THE ROOM
AROUND YOU IS THE CREATION OF GEORGE
ANDREAS MITSUYAGA, OF WHOM YOU
HAVE UNDOUBTEDLY HEARD. MITSUYAGA'S
RESEARCHES ARE DIRECTED PRIMARILY TO
THE CONTROL OF HUMAN CONSCIOUSNESS.
THE THEORY UNDERLYING THESE RE-
SEARCHES IS THAT THE FULL USE OF THE
HUMAN MIND AND, CONSEQUENTLY, THE
FULL USE OF THE HUMAN BODY CAN BEST
BE EFFECTED BY A CONSTANT INWARD-
TURNING, A DEEP EXPLORATION OF THE
WORLD WITHIN YOURSELF. THIS ROOM AND
ITS CONTENTS ARE THE RESULT OF A LIFE-

TIME DEVOTED TO THE PURSUIT OF THIS
GOAL AND, AS YOU PROGRESS THROUGH
THE STAGES OF THE COURSE, YOU WILL DIS-
COVER A GREATER CONTROL OVER YOUR-
SELF AND, CONSEQUENTLY, OVER THE
WORLD AROUND YOU. YOU MUST BE
WARNED AGAIN, AS YOU WERE WARNED
WHEN FIRST INDUCTED INTO THE PRO-
GRAM, THAT THE WAY IS DIFFICULT, THAT
COMPLETE CONCENTRATION IS NECESSARY
TO THE SUCCESSFUL COMPLETION OF THIS
PROGRAM AND, FINALLY, THAT SHOULD
YOU FIND YOURSELF THREATENED BY
YOUR EXPERIENCES IN THIS ROOM, YOU
MUST IMMEDIATELY CEASE THE COURSE
AND REQUEST AID AND STABILIZATION
FROM YOUR COUNSELOR. AGAIN, AS YOU
HAVE BEEN TOLD, THE FINAL STEPS OF THIS
COURSE ARE BASED ONLY ON THEORY
SINCE, AT THE TIME THIS ROOM WAS CRE-
ATED, NOT EVEN MITSUYAGA HAD COM-
PLETED THE ENTIRE PROGRAM. SHOULD
THIS INFORMATION BE OUT OF DATE, YOU
WILL HAVE BEEN INFORMED AND YOU MAY
DISREGARD THIS CAVEAT. NO ONE WILL
DISTURB YOU IN THIS ROOM: YOU MAY
PURSUE THIS COURSE WITHOUT FEAR OF
UNTIMELY INTERRUPTION. HOWEVER, IT IS
YOUR RESPONSIBILITY TO SEE THAT YOUR
MIND AND BODY ARE PROPERLY MAIN-
TAINED. TIMING IS ESSENTIAL. THE STAGES
OF PROGRESS ARE NUMBERED CONSECU-
TIVELY, AND THE LAYOUT OF THIS ROOM
REFLECTS THIS ORDER. BEGIN AT THE NEXT
LOCUS WHEN YOU FEEL READY. THANK
YOU.

The screen resolved into blackness again, and I

grinned at it with contempt. So, the mystery, the darkness, the wonder of the building was resolved simply to this: another of the innumerable attempts of our pre-Shaping ancestors to do in awkward and complicated ways what Lippencott had done so easily, to potentiate the human body, to attain immortality. Lippencott succeeded through rays and chemicals and spirits, others failed through a mystic inner turning of the mind. Idiocy, yet I was curious to discover what particular shapings this present idiocy took. I positioned myself before the next hump of blackness, felt the numeral "1" raised in flocking along its surface, and pressed its silver spot. The same list of languages presented itself; I touched "English" and the list faded, replaced by:

KINDLY RECLINE ON THE COUCH PROVIDED.

I looked behind me, discerned a flattened ridge rising from the floor, and lay upon it, keeping my eyes on the screen. As soon as my entire body rested on the ridge, the words on the screen changed:

PLEASE REMOVE YOUR CLOTHES.

Oh, very well. I stood and stripped, then reclined once more. The sides of the ridge rose gently, reached around my sides and met over my body, leaving only my head free. I clawed and kicked at the bindings, suddenly frightened, but my writhings made no difference in the warm clasp of the material. I fought, then relaxed, catching my breath. The restraints ceased their tightening and encased me with warmth. Calm. Relax. If necessary, I could call the remote to my assistance. Somewhat reassured, I glanced back at the screen.

It was pulsing at me, deep, even blue washes that grew and faded rhythmically, regularly. I watched with some curiosity, waiting for a change, but none came. Beat, fade, rise, fade. Puzzlement. But the movement was somehow familiar, and, struck by a thought, I held my breath. The pulsing ceased, and resumed as I let the air whistle out between my lips.

So, a feedback monitor. I played with it for a while longer, holding my breath, letting it out suddenly, panting, breathing deeply and slowly, and the screen paced me.

A subtle change overcame the blue, a hint of redness that also pulsed, but more rapidly. My heart. My breathing stabilized as I watched this new development and the two colors moved in counterpoint to each other. I reached within and felt my heart pulsing, pushing the blood through me, felt my lungs moving and the singing of oxygen slipping through the lungs' lining into the bloodstream, a familiar, comforting sensation.

A shiver of orange danced rapidly across the screen, and this one I recognized immediately. Alpha waves; these, too, I could regulate. A joining of beta waves, a movement within my mind. The world narrowed to encompass only the screen and my body, more and more colors pulsing and dancing through the one, more and more sensations weaving and interleaving through the other. This, I decided, was nice, this was pleasant. This, at the least, was making the decaying hulk of my body create pretty pictures for my amusement. And I moved more deeply within myself.

What a glorious waste! The almost mystic arrangements and changes all summed to extinction, the end result of this subtle physical mathematic was death, and the equation carried its cessation within its very life. That small prettiness, there, is but the slow migration of calcium from bone to blood; this tiny, bright popping adds to the yearly loss of one gram's worth of brain. An alien wonder, a busy and beautiful other that had, in some malign fashion, attached itself to me, that insisted on making me wither, on making me die. Pain-maker. Infiltrated by plastic parts, subverted by a stubborn mortality. Yet so lovely, so terribly lovely. I reached toward the pulsing enchantment of my heart, and touched it.

Touched it. Changed it. Affected its movements. Altered its pace.

With my—mind? Consciousness? Spirit? Soul?

I approached again, felt its steady flutter, reached for it. Slowed it, and speeded it again. Wonderment. Wonderment. I gasped and molecules within my lungs danced and sang, I leeched oxygen into my bloodstream thickly, richly, cut the flow to a trickle and expanded it once more. Played with the slidings of my intestines, fooled with the tiny valves and tubes of my glands, felt emotions wash over me and pinpointed their causes, captured the scurrying pinpoints of hormones and cancelled them from me. Made my fingernails grow long, shed some skin on my arms, filled my womb with unseasonable blood and reabsorbed it. Touched my brain and microscopic fireworks sparkled through my skull, scenes and scents and tastes long forgotten raced through, tumbled up and over and out and back once more. I heard the sighing of the sea and the slapping of waves leagues away, the soft whisper of electricity moving through the wires of the machine, the tiny interfaces within the remote. Felt the turning of the earth beneath me and the pulling of the tides through the liquids of my body and was, suddenly, no longer the alien, no longer the butt of mortality's joke. I pulsed as the ocean pulsed, joined to it, to the earth, to the pull of the seasons and the changes of the moon. I, me, Tia, body and soul, the creator and that which is created, the wine and its flask, the temple and its door. Beatitude. Joy. Peace. Laughter.

When we came back, the joy and I, the arms of the ridge on which I rested were retracted, and the screen no longer pulsed and moved, but instead displayed the words:

YOU HAVE NOW SUCCESSFULLY COMPLETED YOUR FIRST MONTH'S SESSION IN THE COURSE. COMPLETE REST AND INTEGRATION ARE NOW INDICATED, AND YOU MAY THEN PROGRESS TO THE SECOND STATION.

Twenty-eight days? I asked my body. No, it as-

sured me, no, nothing even close. I rose and inspected
the time-meter on the remote and discovered that no
more than two hours had passed since I activated the
machine. Had the room's mechanisms aged to the
point of unreliability? Somehow I doubted it. Then I
considered the abilities I had brought with me, the
inward-turning and the monitoring, and I understood.
Three-quarters of what the machine sought to teach
me was already old to me, and only the last step was
new.

But that last step.

I had touched. Controlled. Determined. Created
and changed my tiniest drippings and drainings.
Moved my heart. I reached within and changed my
heartbeat again, felt it obedient to my will, then sat,
overwhelmed by what I had done.

⚔ 35 ⚔

The summer I was fourteen years old, my mother and I left our mutual home, she to go her way, to the sandy deserts of Mars, and I to go mine, to Seville and the university. I had my student's allotment and a credit allowance given me as a gift by my father, the second time I met him. I had lost my virginity six months before on a field-float gliding through the hot swamps of the Everglades, had lost it gloriously, thrashing under the slight shimmer of the field that protected our bodies from insects and the sweltering sun.

I journeyed to Seville, picked up my registration cubes, selected my First Field of Study, and found a small apartment above one of the older squares, where I could look out over the carefully restored tile roofs to the spires of a rebuilt cathedral. I soon moved within a circle of other students about my own age, sharing songs and beds. My studies progressed well. My mother and I communicated once or twice during the summer, then she contracted for another child and we lost touch with each other. Summer faded gently into autumn, my classes changed, I knew the campus city by heart, and I flourished.

One of my autumn classes consisted of a laboratory in comparative botany and, since many of the subjects needed an approximation of their native Martian climate to thrive, this class was held old-style—many students meeting twice a week in a large laboratory near the center of the city. This building, too, was a restoration, with huge stone steps leading to its colonnaded portico and arching windows strung along its heavy, grey walls. The portico was a favorite liftplace; it faced a busy plaza and we would thrill ourselves by leaping from between the ornate columns to buzz over the heads of shoppers and passers-by. Complaints were issued and reprimands came down, of course, but nonetheless we could not resist the temptation to soar over the crowd, cartwheeling through the soft Iberian air.

I remained in the laboratory late one day, intent on completing a private grafting project of my own. I wanted to merge a Terran cactus, a Mammilaria Collinsii, and a Martian Bryantia Obesa. I was young, and not in the least bothered by the failure of botanists more gifted than I to accomplish this feat. So I bent over my worktable, completely absorbed, and only looked up when the quality of the light changed. The walls had assumed their evening radiance, and it was long past my normal meal time. My stomach complained as I carefully replaced my instruments, made a few final notes and slipped the graft into a support system. I left the building, shrugged my liftpack over my shoulders and stood a moment on the edge of the portico watching the evening throngs.

They filled the square and the air above it, promenading, eating and drinking at the cafes, in the usual motley assortment of clothing and a sprinkling of nudity. The rays of the setting sun, the radiance of the

walls around the plaza, etched each individual dis-
tinctly, giving each one a separate aura of light and
shadow, brilliance and shade. And, as I stood perched
on the brink of flight, I suddenly perceived the en-
tirety of this multifaceted crowd as something totally
apart from myself, felt the clasp of my own skin and
realized completely and utterly how very alone I was,
how very individual, how wholly contained within the
universe of my own skin. Me, Tia, apart, absolutely
other, myself and no one else, inviolate. The feeling
came over me with all the intensity of an ancient's
meeting with God, a transcendental merging of individual and absolute truth: a feeling not so much of
mind as of the entire being, body, soul, everything. I
stood shaking with the intensity of the vision, and the
shaking transmuted to a sense of growing and glowing
elation, of pristine and absolute joy. I, me, Tia
Hamley, myself. I am sufficient; I am, simply and
beautifully; a purely gratuitous gift. I exist.

I took off from the portico and flung myself into the
most harebrained and madcap aerial arabesques the
city of Seville had seen, ricocheting, laughing, bub-
bling, and diving through the evening air as though
possessed. I shot through the waters of the plaza's
fountains and spun glittering drops around me as I
lifted again. I sat on the spire atop the cathedral and
sang bawdy songs. I stole three oranges from a vendor
and juggled them, laughing hysterically. In short, I
was a disgrace.

Someone complained, of course. I was reprimanded
and my liftpack was removed for a month. But it was
worth it, every single step.

⚔ 36 ⚔

"What the hell did you think you were doing?"

"You should know better than that!"

"Where's the remote? Where's the remote?"

"We had all the remotes hunting for you!"

"If you do something like that again, I'll, I'll have you restricted to the ship!"

The layers of ocean passed by as I rose from my fifty-minute decompression stop toward the dark bulk of the *Ilium* and the bright, illuminated circle of the diving well. The remote tagged along behind me, trailing my sop to Cerbeus: a rusted lamp from the main lobby of Mitsuyaga's building, something to placate the greediness above. As far as the Immortals would ever know, I hoped, the lamp would represent all that was salvageable from the disintegrating, silted, empty and completely mythic building I planned to describe to them. Greville and Harkness continued shouting, their voices pouring through my helmet like small, infuriated gnats. I turned down the volume again and made no reply.

". . . against every safety precaution!"

"You could have been killed!"

"That's valuable equipment!"

I pulled myself up the rungs of the diving well and emerged dripping into the hold while the remote dropped the lamp into the general store and moved to its proper niche. Greville, Harkness and Paul were gathered at the lip of the well, Greville windmilling in excitement, Harkness shouting angrily, Paul staring at me. I popped the plugs from my mask and the voices ceased their attack, but Greville and Harkness continued shouting, their mouths straining and biting noiselessly. I snapped my face-plate open and peeled off the headsheath, dropped them to the floor beside me and sat quietly, legs over the edge of the well, watching the two until their voices faltered and stilled.

"I brought a lamp," I said. "There wasn't much else in there. The remote's back in its locker."

". . . valuable . . ." Greville sputtered.

"I have the usual bond posted," I told him. "You don't have to worry about losing your money."

"But you could have been killed," Harkness protested, making the final word carry all the horror it could hold.

"That's my worry, isn't it? Look, I'm very tired. If you want to talk about this later, fine, but right now I'm going to sleep."

"That," said Greville, "that's fine for you, but I want you to know, I just want you to know, that if you *ever* do that again, I'll have you taken off the ship, I really will."

"Try it," I said. "Remember what the Law says. If you think you can prove that I've damaged or defrauded you, then take it to Berne and I'll contest it. I have an independent contract, remember?"

Greville opened his mouth, then thought better of it and stormed from the room, the hem of his lab coat flapping angrily around his bare thighs and his two-toned bush of hair standing raggedly about his head.

Harkness looked stiffly uncomfortable. "What can I say? We were worried."

"About what?" I snapped. "The remote? Bad karma?"

He shrugged, oddly helpless, and left the hold.

I rose, stripped away my wet-suit and tossed it over by my locker while I went to clean up.

When I returned, the wet-suit had been dried and layered neatly in my locker, and Paul was stacking the rest of my equipment in its proper place.

"You didn't have to do that," I said, surprised.

"I thought you'd be too tired to do it yourself," he said with a smile, and irised the locker's mouth closed. "Can I come up with you?"

"If you want," I said, and led the way to my cabin.

"Was it very dangerous?" Paul asked as we stepped through the door.

"No, not particularly. Why?"

"You were out of contact for so long. We waited for you underwater, then Greville sent the remotes and Tobias said we should come up immediately. Jenny wanted to stay."

"Really?" I stretched out on my hammock, paying only the slightest attention to him. I felt the muscles relax through my body, felt the small tensions drain away; played with my heartbeat for a moment, then explored the doings of my intestines. I could feel the slow accumulation of blood and tissue lining my uterus, the minute secretions of my ovaries, small vibrations through the complexities of my inner ears as Paul continued speaking.

"I thought you might have ripped your suit, that you might have drowned." His voice dropped an octave, reached me husky and dense. "I thought of you lying trapped in rocks with your hoses cut, or impaled by one of those big fish. I thought I saw you floating through the buildings with your face dead behind your mask, or your mask ripped off."

The resonance of his voice drew my attention, and

without opening my eyes I concentrated on his words. His voice moved closer, came now from directly above my face.

"I saw you lying naked on a bed of silt, with sea-plants in your hair and your eyes opened, and tiny fish swimming over your cunt, and your body swayed in the water. I saw you held down by the suckers of an octopus, and it wrapped one tentacle around your breast, like this." His shaking hand cupped my breast, his thumb moved over the seal of my suit, opening it. "And it touched your body, here, and here, leaving bright red circles that turned green over your skin, on your belly, on your thighs, and when it moved to cover you its beak split your skin, but your eyes didn't move because you were dead, Tia, drowned."

Mesmerized, I turned my head to look at him, saw at eye level the stiff red urgency of his cock. One small, translucent drop gathered at the tip and fell shining to the floor as he unsealed the rest of my suit and removed it, as he moved into the hammock, poised himself above me.

"And I saw the tentacles open your thighs, and probe through the tiny green plants that grew between your legs, and I saw it enter you, like this, like, this, all, the, way, in, and it fucked you, Tia, and it, harder, and harder, and, and, but you didn't move, because, because you were *dead!*" He screamed as he came; I could feel the hot spurting within me, the contractions of his cock, the final epileptic thrust that broke my horrified fascination and sent me clawing my way from under him, from the hammock, across the room to turn and stare in shock at his quivering back. He lay gasping, his fingers grabbing the edges of the polycrystal mesh. The entire hammock shook.

I fought to calm the ragged tension within my chest, fought to force words through the constrictions of my throat, through my clenched teeth.

"Get out," I whispered, then, more loudly, "Get out!"

He turned to face me, jaw slack, eyes glazed over, not yet returned from his orgasm. "Tia. . . ."

"Get the death out!" I screamed, grabbed his discarded tunic, threw it at him. "Out! OUT!"

He stumbled from the hammock, his tunic held limply before him. "Tia. . . ."

"OUT!"

He backed from my cabin, staggering, and I slammed my palm against the lock. My body twisted and knotted convulsively, and I fell to the floor, weeping. Somewhere within my spine, the small early twinges of pain began.

37

Greg shed his jumpsuit, impatiently peeling the material from his chest and thighs and tossing it into the cleaner. He used the vibrashower as I keyed through the mail, and by the time I stripped he was stretched out on the pale blueness of the forcebed. I took my time in the shower, clearing off the sticky residue of a day spent walking the line, of an evening checking and rechecking the hydroponic systems aboard the *Outbound*. By the time I re-emerged, Greg had flowed the walls around the bed, cutting the rest of the small apartment from view, and was playing with a tiny, vibrating bottle held in his large hand.

"What's that?" I asked, sitting beside him on the bed.

"Something Kai-Yu gave me. It's from Mars, they call it some untranslatable, unpronounceable word, something they made up. It's supposed to be a Martian religious drug they found in one of the ruins. You

don't believe that, eh? Well, I don't much either, but
Kai-Yu said he tried it and it's good and it's not dangerous. Okay?"

I took the small bottle from him and held it to the
light. It felt cool against my palm, and the liquid
within glowed with a multitude of small, distinct points
of color.

"Why not? Do we drink it or what?"

"We drink it. Let's see, one drop for one hour is
what he said. Two hours, eh? Two for you, two for
me, then we sleep."

I brought two goblets of wine from the small kitchen
space while Greg found a clean pipette. He mixed the
proper dosage, then sealed the small bottle and added
it to our stash in one of the storage units. We toasted
each other solemnly and drank the wine.

Tripping with Greg: we were in the habit of doing it
once or twice a month during the year we'd been together. Always in privacy, and our closeness seemed
to potentiate the drugs we took, boosting not only our
own inner awareness but also our awareness of each
other. We rotated our trips, one time doing a visual
drug, the next a sensory, then one that sprang open
our throats and we would talk for hours, huddled together on our transparent bed. This last type was
my least favorite. I found myself setting censors to my
mind and mouth, still careful to hide the secret of my
mortality. It led to guilt and shame, yet I could not
think of any way around it, of any way to tell him of
my approaching withering and death without destroy-
ing the precious, time-bound love we shared. So I remained silent and took the drug as rarely as I could.

We finished the wine and lay back on the bed. In-
evitably our hands moved to each other's bodies,
mouths joined and parted, and I tasted the textures of
his neck, shoulder, chest, hips, moving through the
convolutions of sharing and love. When we joined I
rode atop him, upright, to watch the changes in his
eyes, or to look down to where our bodies merged,
wondering again at the perfect fit we always seemed to

manage. We were so involved that we didn't notice
the onset of the trip until we came, I for the second
time. Greg said in a conversational voice, "Little one,
this is a very funny come," while his hips arched below me in orgasm. I couldn't reply. Thick waves of
ecstasy moved through me, reaching from my center
to encompass every cell, every nerve ending, until I
could not distinguish between my body and my body's
sensations. And it seemed to last forever, to catapult
me up and over the confines of my body. I floated,
became a merging of sensations without any physical
ground, both in the midst of, and myself creating, a
warm and pulsing void.

Time became tactile, a moving entity twisted back
on itself, a visual presence shot through with long
greens along its path, cool and solemn through my
fingers and through my skin. I and the serpent of
time, one and inseparable, moved sweeping through
the universe, swallowing lemon-flavored suns and ex-
creting dissonances of novae; ten thousand discrete
rivulets of coolness traveled along our moving skins.
The quick, sharp scents of light and shadow amid the
serpent smoothness, a smell of red, a tinge of slow, a
rushing of bittersweet galaxies, unattainable, mysterious, beautiful, amid the bongings and twangings and
hummings and keenings as I and the serpent brushed
the strings of the universe; canticles of eternity, har-
monies of light, the sharp piccolo colors of meteors
and comets, and the quickness of planets and suns. O,
wondrous, this; dappled and drenched, delight and
desire.

I am an infinitely tiny point of light amid the huge-
ness of the stars and emptiness I have myself created.
Where? How? Who? Why? The universe laughs, gusts
of merriment and I am nothing to it, void, emptiness,
drop to ocean but apart, mote to mountain but different; I am crushed, engulfed, drowned in indifference.

It's only a drug only a trip only a dream I am, I
am, I am, I am. . . .

Lying in my room. With walls about me. Secure.

Snug. Safe. Certain. Peace, and the serpent foiled. I raise my hand, laughing, in victory.

My hand is bone. The skin lies over it like a thin, semi-opaque membrane, fingers as strands of fine wire, thick knobs on skinny wrists, mottled, dank, dry. Skin in slack folds over arms, shoulders, abdomen; my breasts are two scaly, empty bags suspended from sharp and twisted shoulders. Legs buckle and twist, welted with thick, protruding blue veins. I raise my hands to my face, feel the icy wetness of spittle running from pinched lips, harshness of hair on pointed chin and the hooked barb of my nose, collapsing with the weight of age toward my mouth. No! NO! The sound is the sound of my screams; the pain is the sharpness of fingernails digging through flesh; the scent is the scent of fear. *This is not me! This is not me!*

The screams awaken hands that rest on my broken body, strong, strong, with the warmth of youth, and they have come to dispose of me, rid themselves, take me. Take me where? How? Into the disposal system; into the secret, terrifying coldness of morgues, into a zoo, into a zoo. I scream, I scream, until the universe is suddenly, painfully sucked into blackness and I am left solitary in an infinity of dead suns.

I came back suddenly, and as my eyes opened Greg cried my name and turned me in his arms to face him.

He was wrapped around me, starfish, his face strained and anxious as I fought from his grasp and staggered across the room, keyed the reflecting screen. My image leaped out at me—light, lithe, rounded, firm, with only the staring emptiness of the eyes to remind me of what I had been. Would be. Greg caught me in his arms as I slumped against the screen, cradled me, and carried me back to the bed.

"Tia, little one, Tia, you are all right now? You are back here? Yes? Tia?"

Love and strength, warmth and protection. I leaped from his comfort, sank my back against the far wall and faced him as he sat, bewildered, amid the blueness of the bed.

"I'm going to die," I whispered, and, louder, "I'm going to die, Greg."

"But little one, we are all going to die, eventually, one way or another. Come back to bed."

"No, you don't understand. I'm going to die, I'm going to get old and wrinkled and ugly, and then I'm going to die!"

"No, I do not understand. Tia, what is this? Is it your trip still?" He glanced at the timepiece on the wall.

"No, Greg, beloved, listen. They didn't work, the Treatments didn't work on me, at all, nothing. . . ."

"This I do not believe. You are still tripping, I gave you too much, it is my fault. Come, sleep, it will soon be over." He smiled, worried and opened his arms to me.

The comsystem, here, next to me. I forced my hands to stop shaking long enough to punch for and authorize my records from the Treatment Center, gathered the print-out together and offered it to my lover.

"Here. Read it."

"No. Tia, it is late. We will sleep, this will pass, here, come." He took the sheets from my hands, dropped them on the floor without glancing at them, then carried me once more to the bed, and lay wrapped around me. His refusal to consider my mortality seemed to me the cruelest joke of all, and I lay still, defeated, within the circle of his arms.

Time passed, and when he thought I slept he rose, gathered the papers and read them by the dim glow of one light globe. The sheets rustled as, one by one, he finished with them and let them fall. Eventually he came to bed again, gathered me in his arms and rocked us both. I felt a small, surprising wetness where his face pressed against my neck.

When he slept soundly, I slipped from the bed, tossed my clothes in a bag and crossed to the door. Then, on impulse, I retrieved Kai-Yu's stoppered bot-

tle from storage and added it to my bag. Ran across
the early morning dome to the station, caught a train
for Luna and spent the next ninety minutes with my
mind as blank as the landscape outside the tube.

Deep within my body, for the first time, a small
pain began.

38

I wasn't able to sleep that night, haunted by the glaze of Paul's eyes, by stray horrors unwillingly remembered from the past, by impending dooms awaiting me beyond next year's sunrises. I spent the night huddled in the vacant minaret, my orange blanket tucked around me, sleeplessly watching the distant stars, unwilling to return to the new discomforts of my cabin.

My back betrayed me in the night, but I impatiently pushed the pain from me, too miserable to take joy in my easy victory over my body. Just before dawn, I gave up all pretense of sleep, left the orange blanket lying on the floor of the minaret and crept down to the galley to make coffee and rolls. A small light shone through the galley door, and I found Jenny sitting at the worktable, alone, bent over a cup of coffee. She raised her head from her hands at my entrance, half startled, and the look she gave me was almost one of relief.

"Morning," I said. "Can I have some coffee?"

She nodded wearily and rested her forehead in her palms again. Her black hair was tumbled and mussed, eyes ringed darkly. I filled a cup, rummaged through the pantry for a roll and, finding one, crossed the galley to slip it through the oven. As I passed her, she held out her cup.

"More, please?"

I refilled the cup, placed it before her, and went back to the oven. I hadn't intended to stay, but it was hard to ignore her misery, much as I was locked into my own. Instead of taking the coffee and roll back to the minaret, I set them on the table, pulled up a stool, and sat across from her.

"Hard night?" I asked.

She nodded, sighed, massaged the back of her neck with long fingers. "Tobias is upset. He locked himself in his cabin last night, won't let me near him."

I sipped the coffee, watching her.

"After you came back, yesterday, he just seemed to go to pieces," she said, and I shook my head.

"I don't want to hear about it, Jenny. Please. I've enough problems already."

"That's what you always say," she said bitterly. "You have problems, he has problems, everyone has problems and no one's willing to do anything about them."

"I'm not Tobias' keeper."

"Tia, please, can't you try to understand? He's not what you think, he's got reasons, he, I mean. . . ." Her hands chased words through the air, unable to capture the right ones.

"Do you love him?"

"Love him?" She looked startled. "I don't know, I haven't thought about it. . . ."

"Then why the constant worry? If he wants to be an unreasonable bastard, that's his business, not yours. And not mine."

"But you can't turn your back on him. . . ."

"Listen, if he wants anything from me, he can ask.

And he's made it obvious that he doesn't need anything I'd be willing to give him. Stop trying to make me sympathetic to him, Jenny, it just won't work."

"Don't you care about anybody?" she cried.

"Not if I can avoid it."

"Not even Paul?"

I almost dropped the cup. "Paul? Care about Paul? Let me tell you about Paul, child. Just let me tell you. . . ." And I did, against all reason, in pain and fury. She stared at me in rising bewilderment, in rising sickness, but I could not stop myself, not until I'd told her everything, every last detail, and she stopped my recitation with a scream, grabbed her hair and pulled it hard. I leaped to my feet, rounded the table, took her by the shoulders, and shook her with all my strength.

"What now? Shocked? Sick? What now, Jenny? Afraid he might have done it to you?" I forced the words through clenched teeth, shaking her until her hair flew around her stiff face. "Do you empathize with *that,* Jenny?"

I shoved her down and she fell across the table, crying. I turned to leave, but—

"Tia!" she cried.

She pushed herself up from the table and stared at me. Tears gleamed and puddled in her eyes, and she whispered, "I'm no different than he is."

"Are you, then?" I hissed. My hand rose to the seam of my clingsuit, but she screamed, pushed away from the table with such force that she toppled it, and ran down the corridor. I stared at the upended table, racked between fury and tears, then turned and fled to the sanctuary of the minaret.

39

At ten that morning the Immortals gathered on the mosaic deck below my tower to divide the previous day's plunder. Several floaters loaded with loot appeared and hovered in the center of the deck, while the Immortals stood in a ragged semi-circle before them, and Greville began the division.

Random words floated up to me through the warm air as Greville displayed each object. Long, asinine lectures on each item, things wrongly identified, pompousness of various forms and shades, then the bidding and bickering over each piece. Hart, as usual, bid for himself and for Harkness, who remained on the bridge. Benito, as usual, was absent, down in the engine room with his beloved monsters, and no one bid for him. Jenny did not appear, but Paul automatically bid on everything, and gleaned for himself a great hulking pile of junk.

Oh, Lord. Plastic building blocks, models of hover-cars and moonshuttles, wrappings to fit over infants' diapers. Plastic jars with thin, arching protrusions, rubber spheres, plastic head-protectors, ovals of metal with handles affixed to one end. Perfume bottles of cut glass, lotion jars, plastic hats, combs, brushes, bent wires for holding hair in place, a vibrating cup for cleaning prosthetic teeth. The chandelier. Belt buckles. Shoe-horns. Skeletons of lamp shades. Push-carts. Metal drain-stoppers, crusted and oozing. Rusted keys. An onyx egg. Plastic dolls. And more, and more, until I grew sick of the accumulations and quietly came down from my tower, avoided the deck and made my way to Benito's cave.

"What do you want?" he demanded as I approached him. He had moved a large generator from its place in line and was struggling to unlock one of the housing plates.

"Thought I'd give you a hand."

"Don't need one," he grunted and turned his back to me. He groped for a tool on a floater beside him, and I picked up the implement and handed it to him.

"Look, I'm sorry about. . . ."

"Doesn't matter."

"Come off it, Benito. Can't I even apologize?"

"No. Go back to your great romance, I don't need your help."

The words refused to come, stuck in my throat with the other horrors of the night before. I shook my head helplessly, sat on a heavy conduit and rested my forehead in my palms, waiting for the sudden nausea to pass.

A quick clatter, and when I raised my head Benito had slammed his tools down on the floater, snapped the plate back into suspension and was stalking down the lines of the generators toward his own inviolate cabin. He turned briefly as he reached the door to glare at me.

"Go to Australia!" he shouted, and snicked the port closed behind him.

The nausea redoubled, but I forced it down, stood, and walked slowly through the glimmering machines.

⚔ 40 ⚔

When the Immortals were finished dividing the loot, I floated the remains to the Museum and set about cataloging each piece.

The ship's collection was housed in a long, echoing gallery with mirrors along one side and high, arched windows along the other. The upper quarter of each window was programmed to a different hue, and the lights reflected off the mirrors and created patches of color along the floors and walls; at night, radiance spilled in from just outside and above the arches, so that at any time of the day the room seemed to be filled with clear sunlight.

The exhibits were stored in low cases along the sides of the gallery. Each item floated within a clear, protective bubble provided with a small, transparent band along its lower end that, when activated, read out a brief description of the piece. I had, in my three years with the *Ilium,* managed to correct many

of the descriptions and to identify most of the items on
display. But there was much left to do, and each new
dive added to the job. Too many of the cases were
identified only by the year the item was found and a
question mark. The Museum seemed to remind the
Immortals of how much they had accrued; it reminded
me of how much I had yet to learn.

That day's pickings were lean. Most of the items
duplicated things the Museum already had, and I
tagged them for storage and eventual sale to other
collections. A few items were unique; the best was a
set of pens preserved in a clear plastic block, with a
plaque affixed to one side. The plaque was corroded
beyond legibility, but I thought it probable that the
pens were used to sign some historic document. They
were the best preserved specimens we had found to
date, and I created a niche for them in the gallery and
labelled them properly.

The afternoon passed undisturbed, and I deliberately made it so, kept my mind far from Paul, from
Benito, and would not allow one thought unconnected
with my sorting and labelling. These tasks done, I
requested music from the computer and guided one of
the vacant floaters to a window, curled up on it and
watched the water lapping gently at the sides of the
ship, beyond and below the thin, arching lines of the
outer railings. The Museum was on the first deck up
from the water-line, and the water was very close.

I closed my eyes and reached within myself once
more for the first time since last night, half fearful that
my new-found abilities had vanished. But my body
responded to my gentle pokings and, escaping Paul,
Benito, Immortals, *Ilium* and all, I settled down to a
testing and exploration of myself.

Time passed quietly during my absorption. I
learned to leech certain things from my stomach into
my bloodstream, learned to distinguish the commands
that effectuated one action rather than another. I felt
the slight beginnings of certainty as my control in-
creased, and I took time from my explorations for a

small wash of satisfaction. Me, Tia Hamley, I can do it.

My solitude was broken by a high, horrified keening that filled the gallery and pierced through the layers of my concentration. It catapulted me up and out of the floater on which I lay. The scream came again and again, from the speakers high in the ceiling of the room.

"Who is it?" Harkness' voice shouted over the terror. "Where are you?"

Screams, unbroken by any attempt to speak.

"What?" Greville's voice yelled. "What? Stop it! Stop it!"

"I command you to. . . ."

"Everyone shut up!" The voice was steady and controlled. It took me a moment to recognize it as Jenny's. "Quiet! Greville, Harkness, shut up! Now stop screaming. Stop. We'll come to help as soon as you tell us where you are. Calm down. Quiet. Stop. Where are you? Everything will be all right, but you must calm down. Just tell us where you are, we'll come, but you *have* to tell us where you are."

The screaming modulated and the screamer managed to gasp "the hold, the gen. . . ." before falling back into terror.

I shrank the floater, threw myself atop it and goosed the jets, streaking from the Museum toward the nearest dropshaft. The generator hold was two levels under and its entrance lay on the other side of the *Ilium;* I moved as fast as I could, but the rest of them had reached the hold before me and stood grouped, frozen, near the central platform as I leaped from the floater and hurried toward them.

The screams had stopped. Lonnie stood shaking hysterically near the edge of the group, the large red mark of a hand across one cheek and half-hidden under her stiff, upraised fingers. As I came closer she turned and hid her face against Paul's shoulder; although his arm rose automatically to circle her shoulders, he remained staring at something before him.

Jenny stood close by, staring also, and Tobias retched against the bulk of a machine. The rest were as statues, frozen in the act of seeing the Gorgon, and I had to elbow and push my way between them until I, too, could see.

Benito lay sprawled over the generator, hands flung outwards as though he had leaped atop the large, naked machine. The discarded plate rested against a side of the machine, amid a scatter of tools, and I could see a complexity of wiring between his outspread legs. His feet dangled above the floor, unmoving.

"Benito?" I said.

"He turned off the machine," Hart said, forcing the words from his throat. "Lonnie and I helped him bring it over, and took off the the the plate, and when we, we got back from the sorting, he, he turned it off, and, and, turned it off and went to fix fix fix but the ch, charge, no time, and he took off the, off the, wires and it built up and he, and he. . . ."

And he threw himself over the power beam. I looked above the generator, up at the main cooling line that the beam should have severed, bathing the hold in liquid oxygen, freezing the delicate mechanisms of the control platform and crippling the ship. But the cooling line was intact because Benito had blocked it, had taken and dissipated the full force of the beam with his body.

After the sorting. After, then, our argument. Angry, impatient, it wasn't like Benito to forget to check for a charge build-up. Impatient. Careless. Because we had argued, he made a mistake, and because he made a mistake, he was . . . dead.

No one moved, and my hands remained frozen to my sides. The *corpse* needed lifting, the *dead man* must be settled. *It,* and it filled me with horror. This was no cat, no animal. This was a human, one of me. Was Benito.

Was Benito. His name loosened my hands, and I walked to the generator, reached up and held him by the waist. Only a momentary hesitation, then I held firm, pulled him gently to the floor and turned him over. His face was still there, the scarred lips firmly clasped together, but the front of his shirt bore a clean, sharp puncture. As I rested his body on the floor, a bright red bulge poked through the aperture and his hump made a soft, squishing sound as it collapsed.

Behind me Greville, Harkness, Li and Hart fled the hold, and Paul started to vomit.

⪻ 41 ⪼

Remember Duval? Duval pursues butterflies in Southern Africa, Maya's making sonic sculpture on Mars, George just left for Moscow to become a doctor. Fuad has learned to fly space shuttles, Valentine continues drinking in Paris, Tai-li will be raising Victor's baby, Benito is dead.

Remember Helene? Helene finished her dissertation on relativity, Pyotr dances ballet, Angelique drives sand-cats on Mars. Mabooi designed a new orbiting hotel, Blair's fallen in love, Helmut will be singing opera in Athens, Paul dives from the *Ilium,* Benito is dead.

Remember Lars? Lars weaves cloth in London, Arieh just reached his village in the Pyrenees, Joanna will be applying for a job in the observatories. Satyajit plays theremin for Symphonia Roma, Paulita starts teaching in Seville, Katrina continues in transition, Aureliano builds furniture, Ian sails the Atlantic, Kyoshi makes cheese, Carina argues her case in Berne, Axel has had a baby, Sze-Ya shall search for gold on Diemos.

Benito is dead.

42

It is not easy to lose oneself in Luna. It is, despite its complexity, a small city, an intimate city, and people remember your face. I disembarked at the Library station and stood by the moving belts, wondering where to go, what to do. My change of location had been automatically relayed to the comsystem when I'd purchased the ticket to Luna; the records left by my use of water allotments, transportation, food, would pinpoint me exactly, and I was terrified that Greg or one of his companions would come to find me, would try to take me back to where I so desperately wanted to be. If Greg found me, if he said, "Come back, it doesn't matter, come with us," I would go immediately, forgetting the varieties of hell that going would entail, forgetting what I would be in twenty years or fifty, forgetting that if I indeed loved him as much as I did, then I loved him enough to spare him what I would become.

I shouldered my bag and set out on foot from the
station, using the slidebelts only when I couldn't find
a place to walk, moving aimlessly about the city. The
dome of the city slowly exchanged its nighttime softness for the pink and gold glow of dawn, and gradu-
ally people began to fill the streets, first those whose
jobs demanded an early rising, then the majority of
the city's workers, crowding the slidebelts and swirling
about me as I wandered through the business section
of the city. A number of small cafes and restaurants
were open, serving plates of food from which rose
appetizing odors, but I wandered past each one, rarely
pausing for more than a glimpse inside their clean in-
teriors. The crowds lessened, then, in mid-morning,
thickened again as shoppers ventured out. Tourists
from Terra and Mars appeared with their guide-tapes
and holocameras, dressed in the transparent body-
sheaths and stiff spherical capes of current fashion.
The moon's natives were easy to spot amid the visitors,
for they wore, if anything, fashions ten years out of
date, glimmer-cloth and meters of hair. I still wore the
plain blue clingsuit I had pulled on in Greg's apartment the night before, and strove for the appearance
of an observatory worker on leave. I succeeded, for
the natives did not see me at all, and the tourists gave
me only the same attention given the rest of the city.
I walked through the second level and through the
third, avoiding the location of my old apartment,
barely noticing my surroundings.

By mid-afternoon I found myself back on the first
level of Luna, uncomfortably hungry, uncomfortably
sleepy. My stomach overrode my desire to hide, and
I found a small cafe, ordered a simple meal, and
waited patiently while the machines in the kitchen
buzzed and hummed, preparing my food.

A woman at the next table glanced at me, then
glanced again. I stared out the window at the crowds,
hoping that she would disappear, but she came to my
table and cleared her throat. Reluctantly, I looked up
at her.

"Oh, excuse me, but aren't you from Clarke? I'm sure you are, I was there last week and someone pointed you out, said you were one of the linewalkers. I'm sure I remember you. I've never met a linewalker before."

"No, I'm sorry, you must be mistaken," I said nervously. "I'm from Gagarin, I've just been visiting, I've never been outside."

I must have protested too much, because she smiled. "I'm almost positive I saw you on Clarke, and I don't usually confuse faces. It's my business. Do you mind if I join you?"

I shook my head, miserable, and she sat beside me. "I'm from TeraDisPlays, maybe you've seen my show?"

"No, I don't watch much. Oh, excuse me, here's my meal."

She continued to smile brightly while the plates were placed before me. My hunger effectively routed any manners I had, and I pounced on the food.

"You must be very hungry."

"What?" I said around a mouthful of salad. "Excuse me. No, I just skipped breakfast is all."

"Take your time, then," she said, smiling still. I glanced at her and the meaning of that smile began to dawn on me.

Well, why not? She'd have a room somewhere, registered in her own name, and that would take care of one of my problems. I probably looked to her like one of the young vagabonds that flitted from planet to planet to moon, perpetually broke and perpetually on the move. Broke I certainly wasn't; my balance at Luna City Trust was more than adequate, but the guise of vagabond served my purposes. So I returned her smile and ate more slowly, listening to her talk.

She free-lanced for TeraDisPlays, doing interviews, travel tapes, whatever she found interesting. She'd been on the moon two months and was returning to Beijing in a week, having, or so she said, exhausted the possibilities of the moon. She made one or two more comments about linewalkers, but when I didn't react she let the topic alone. I listened, smiled, volunteered only my name, which she would have discovered anyway.

"Well," she said over coffee, "if you've just come in from Gagarin, you'll probably want to clean up. I have a room not far from here."

Indeed she did. TeraDisPlays must have paid her very well, for the room was one of the most expensive in Luna's most expensive hotel and contained all the latest refinements, including emotion-keyed wall fields that, as I stepped from the sumptuous bathroom, were deep red. The woman lay naked on the bed, idly waiting for me, so I went to her and paid for my bed and board. When she finally let me, I fell asleep.

When I awoke it was near nightfall, and she was dressed and impatient to go out. I soon lost my fear that Greg would find me, for he would never consider searching for me in the gaudy and expensive restaurant and nightclubs where we passed the evening. I drank when drinks were placed before me, danced when dancing was requested, laughed when it seemed appropriate, let myself be passively moved from one activity to another until, after two early morning hours spent thrashing about on her bed, she was finally sated and slept. I lay beside her, tired beyond the point of sleep, while the small traitor hidden in my brain told me that this was no better a solution to my problems than any other, that I had sold myself, compounded one lie with another, presented a face to her that was not my own. It made no difference whether that face was pleasing to her or not, for it was still a fraud, and so was I as long as I wore it. Badgered and nagged, I dragged myself from the bed.

She slept on while I bathed, gathered my bag, and left the hotel room; passed through the almost-deserted lobby and into the darkened streets. The tourist district around the hotel was bright and alive, even at four in the morning, but the smaller streets, the business and residential districts, were dim and quiet. I considered the faces of the buildings as I walked, considered the people within. They slept well, these incompatible compatriots of mine, each secure in the knowledge of a calm forever, as unchanging as they themselves were unchanging. And these were the people who would stare and giggle at me as I grew more and more obviously the freak, would compound my misery with their stares, pointings, talk and, perhaps, their fears. And how would I react? By selling my ugliness to them, as I had sold my attractiveness the day before? By auctioning off an evening with Tia the Hag, something to talk about at parties two centuries hence? For all their melodrama and bathos, the questions were real and bothered me. No, I decided, I would have none of it. Let them find their freaks elsewhere, as I would find some life for myself elsewhere. Tia Hamley was resigning the position of pet monstrosity. Tia Hamley, without Australia, would cope.

And I did. Johns-Rastegar Research Center needed someone to mind the solar observatory—five years alone orbiting the sun, holos and telefaxes, complete computer tie-ins, simulators, good pay, no previous experience necessary. They'd been looking for someone for two years, and took me without a fuss. A week after I'd left Clarke I and my bedraggled pack were shunted up to the station and immured in solitude.

During my second year at the solar station I watched the *Outbound* move from the moon toward the sun, circle our little star, gain momentum, and fling herself out into the blackness of space.

I almost opened the hatch and walked out after her.

43

I sat in the diving hold, legs dangling over the lip of the well, and a scant meter from my feet the water pulsed slowly, gurgling against the sides of the well and gleaming on the transparent doors of the remotes' storage niches. The scent of salt floated up and mingled with the scent of rubber and powder from my mask and wet-suit, lying behind me on the floor where I had discarded them soon after beginning an unnecessary cleaning. Over and under these scents lay the smell of the hold, metal and polish, and beneath me the floor vibrated gently.

Paul was locked in his cabin, presumably coping with Benito's death in his own way, and I refused to consider it further. Lonnie and Li slept, deeply sedated; Harkness was undoubtedly comforting Hart in a familiar manner and Tobias, accompanied as always by Jenny, had taken over Benito's functions in the generator hold until a full engineer could be flown to us from the mainland. I had left them in the hold soon after the others fled, made the call to the mainland and came to the diving hold. I tried to fill my mind with cleaning my equipment and left the job half-done—various implements lay scattered beside and behind me on the floor.

I picked up my faceplate and lay down on the floor, pressing the coolness against my skin, feeling the rasp of my suit's material across my belly and thighs, and the chill puckered my nipples. The faceplate covered one hand, and I looked at it blankly, feeling guilty.

After all, it was my fault, wasn't it? If I hadn't argued with Benito, he would not have been angry, would have been calm enough to consider the possibility of a charge building up in the machine, would have checked, would still be alive. Yet I had gone to him seeking reconciliation, and he had refused it. Was it my fault? I had not pushed him over that generator, nor had I courted his anger. But if we hadn't argued. . . . And why had we argued? Why had Benito been so upset at my liaison with Paul, and why had I let myself react to his anger? And, ultimately, did it even matter? For Benito was dead, and no amount of blame or questioning would change that. The guilt became a quiet, thorough mourning—the only mourning, I suspected, that Benito would get.

"Tia?"

I turned my head and saw Greville standing hesitantly at the foot of the dropshaft.

"Tia, I uh, I need your help." He ventured a few feet further into the room, twisting a button of his lab coat between his fingers. The button came off and he stared at it with dismay, then put it in his pocket.

"Go away, Greville."

"Tia, please, you're the only one who can help."

"Go away."

"It's Benito."

I sat and faced him. "Go on."

"Well, everyone's locked themselves up, everyone

but you and me, and, well . . ." He stalled, started on another button.

"Where's Tobias?"

"He put everything on automatic and he's locked up too. He says he won't go near the generator hold until, as long as, as Benito's, as long as, is down there."

"You mean no one's moved Benito's body yet?"

"Well, who would move it?" he demanded, tugging at the button.

"Greville, just what do you want me to do?"

"Get rid of it! We simply can't have it aboard, don't you see? Get rid of it!"

I thought of Benito, lying alone in the humming room, and stood.

"Okay, Greville."

"Thank you," he called over his shoulder as he ran to the lift-tube.

"Die off," I said to his ascending heels.

Tobias had managed to cover the broken generator on all sides save the one nearest Benito, but no one had covered Benito at all. He lay as I had left him, arms along his sides, legs slightly open, head at an angle. His hump was completely gone now, pushed up through his chest and puddled, sticky, along the floor. He looked very small in death, much smaller than he should have. And cold. I left the generator hold, took my orange blanket from the minaret, and brought it back.

I prepared a pail of soap and water and cleaned Benito's chest, wiped the blood and tissue from him, and cleaned the sticky puddle from the floor. I'd never handled a corpse before, and through my numbness I suddenly remembered Sal, digging a grave with brusque tenderness under the hot Australian sun. It made it easier to wrap Benito in the orange blanket. I tucked the ends in carefully and brought a floater from storage. He was cold, heavy, and inert in my arms as I rolled him onto the floater, positioned him, and rechecked the tightness of the blanket. I paused, my mind moving slowly, then activated the floater and took Benito to the diving hold.

I loaded all my extra, archaic weights onto a spare belt and placed it around Benito's waist. The hold echoed faintly with the clacking of lead on lead as I arranged the belt and cinched it tight, and the air smelled, still, of salt, water, and powder. I looked about for something else, something more, but could not think of anything further.

"Come to the funeral," I said into the intercom by the dropshaft. I sat beside Benito and, after a while, rested my hand on the blanket, over Benito's shoulder. Water slapped against the side of the well.

Someone dropped from the lift-tube. It was Tobias, and I was still so numb that I was not even surprised. He hesitated, then carefully walked around the perimeter of the hold and down toward me, stopping well away. He held his hand out.

Sitting in his palm was Benito's tiny sculpture. It swayed and ticked with the trembling of Tobias' hand, and I looked from the sculpture to Tobias' face. The skin around his mouth was white and taut, and his eyes were rimmed with red.

"I thought," he said, and hesitated. The sculpture shivered. "I thought he might want this."

He tensed as I approached him, but let me take the toy from his hand. We both stared down at it.

"Is it always this way?" Tobias whispered.

I couldn't answer.

"Tia—will this happen to you?"

"I hope not," I whispered.

"Or me?"

I looked up, startled. His voice was hard.

"No, not to me," he continued, and backed away. "I won't let it, and you can't make me."

I shook my head. His face looked like that of the Australian madman. "Tobias, please. Can't we call a truce? Can't we at least not be enemies?"

"No," he said, his voice cold and distant. "No.

You're a freak, Tia. I'm not." He raced toward the lift-tube and jumped up it without hesitation.

I took the small toy and carefully tucked it into the orange blanket beside Benito. I didn't understand why Tobias had brought it, but did understand, vaguely, that Tobias was insane. It didn't matter. All that really mattered, now, was Benito's still shape, and the absence of anything to say to it.

How do you make up a funeral service for a dead Immortal? Sal had said nothing. What do you say to a hunchback? I tried to remember some of the things I had read years ago in the Library; only tiny snatches came to me, but nothing proper, nothing cohesive. So, finally, I said nothing, touched the blanket once, and tilted Benito over the side of the diving well. He sank swiftly, a few bubbles marking the path of his descent, and that was that.

I heard a moist moan behind me, but when I turned all I could see was the lower part of Paul's body, moving swiftly up the column of the lift-tube.

44

"You're out of your mind!" Greville announced. I ignored him and continued shimmying into my wetsuit, as he shifted unhappily from foot to foot, wringing his hands. Tobias and Jenny entered the hold as I sealed my wrist-bands.

"Tia, do you have to. . . ." Jenny asked. I ignored her, too, but Tobias watched in silence, then strode to his locker and began assembling his bubble equipment.

"My God, not you too!" Greville said. "Do you know what you're doing?"

Tobias' full lips puckered in a sullen pout and he refused to answer. Greville, almost frantic, fairly danced.

"One field's already blown, yours might too," he said, his voice rising to a squeak. "It's a great risk, a very great risk!"

"I'll take it," Tobias muttered. "If she can go down, so can I."

"Tobias. . . ." Jenny began.

"I said I'm going down!" he shouted. "Just leave me in peace, will you?"

Jenny shook her head and stormed toward the lift-tube, anger apparent in the stiffness of her back. I shrugged and continued checking my recycler.

"Tia, please. . . . Tobias, this is insane. . . ."

No, I thought. Tobias is insane. But we continued our separate duties in silence, and Greville tossed his hands to his hair in exasperation and left the hold. I wondered briefly why Tobias was coming under, and pushed the question aside. I could lose him, under water. I could travel far faster than he.

Paul appeared as I pulled the rubber smooth around my legs. He stood gnawing at his lower lip.

"Tia, you're not really diving, are you?"

I hoisted my belt and sealed it in place, adjusting the weights until they rested evenly about my hips.

"Greville says it's dangerous," he offered.

Waist beam here. Stunner. Knife. Specimen bags. Chronometer. Depth gauge. Compass. Wrist beams. Remote box. Emergency bubble. Dye. Buoys. Inflatable life jacket. Gloves.

"Something might happen."

I turned to him finally, remembering two nights ago in my cabin, remembering the wet moan that had accompanied Benito's descent to the ocean, fighting nausea. Paul flushed, his gaze leaping from one object to another in the hold, his fingers searching for something on his smooth, naked hips to grasp and, failing that, twisting around each other behind his back. Of course, of course. Not Benito's body, but the orange bundle that represented Benito's body; not Tia's death, but the symbols of that death, the tension of anticipation, the tension of thought. Necrophilia at one remove, the symbol rather than the substance, the shroud and not the corpse. I spread the head-sheath and slipped it over my greying hair.

"Go away, Paul," I said, and he turned and sprinted across the emptiness of the hold and up the shaft.

Tobias sealed my headsheath, then turned around and I completed the hook-up of his waist-band. When Lonnie failed to appear we took the checklists from their place and ran through them carefully.

As we finished and approached the lip of the well, Harkness' voice floated from the intercom.

"I think you're both insane," he said curtly, "but I won't let you go down without some monitoring. I take it you've gone through the safety checks?"

"Yes," I said.

"Very well, then. I've keyed all the remotes for you. . . ."

"I only need one."

"I want them all," Tobias announced, and I shrugged.

"All of them are going, anyway," Harkness said. "Tobias, you might as well start."

He hesitated at the lip of the well, as though remembering the last thing that had slipped into the sea, then set his jaw and climbed down to the water. I waited until his bubble finished forming and he moved to one side, then snapped my face-plate closed and followed him into the ocean.

The current would, by now, have swept Benito's body far from the ship, but I nonetheless maintained a watchful, tense quiet as we descended, and Tobias appeared to share it. A bulky object wavered in the distance, and Tobias started, then had the remotes flood it with light—a bed of kelp. A shark floated alongside us, and swam contemptuously away through the translucent water. We sank slowly through the realm of fading colors, down toward Hilo.

"How are you doing?" Harkness asked.

"All right," I replied. "We're over the business district. A fair amount of destruction on the beach side, probably tsunamis, that sort of thing. A couple of things intact on the inland side of the main street, hard to tell what they are from this distance. Tobias, you want to take a look?"

"Yes," he said. The regiment of remotes dove in response to his signal, and we followed until we hovered before what looked to have been a department store.

"Building's intact," Tobias said. "I'll meter stress in a moment. It looks all right."

"Rich pickings," I commented. Tobias looked at me through the slight shivering of his bubble, then turned back to the building, metered the stress and, after Harkness' go-ahead, had a remote clear a window.

"Go on in," he said to me.

"No, thanks. I think I'll take a look around there." I waved my arm in the direction of Mitsuyaga's building. "You'll have enough help with the remotes, and I only need one."

"Tia," Harkness said, "as Captain, I think. . . ."

"No. Look, I don't want to waste time arguing about this. Just say I'm exercising my independent discovery option and let me get on with it, will you? If Tobias doesn't want to be left all by his lone, he can key one of the remotes to safety, or go back to the ship. I didn't ask for his company." I signalled a remote, opened my jets, and streaked away.

"There she goes!" Tobias yelled. My jets easily outdistanced his bubble. I reached the building and was about to enter before I remembered the remote. It followed me valiantly but, as usual, slowly, and close behind it came Tobias and his own regiment of remotes.

"Tia, wait," Tobias called. "I'm on private band. I have to talk with you."

I slowed down, remembering Benito's toy in Tobias' shaking hand. I reached through the wavering mosses of the doorway and touched the frame, steadying myself against the faint pull of the current, and signalled my remote to enter the lobby and wait for me. As Tobias came closer, I toggled my own transmitter to the privacy band.

"Well?"

He brushed golden hair from his forehead. I couldn't make out his expression through faceplate, water, and the bubble-wall, but the movement of his hands seemed hesitant, and his body, laced with the dark colors of the wires and electrodes, moved like that of a troubled and frightened demigod.

"Tobias," I said, more gently. "What do you want?"

"I don't know," he said. "I—I'm afraid of you."

I laughed, startled, and he tensed angrily. "Of me?" I said, and laughed again.

"It's not funny! You don't belong with us, you don't blend. You make people uncomfortable. And you're a—I mean, bad things happen when you're around. Like Benito."

"You mean I'm a jinx," I said, and turned to go in.

"No! Please, wait. I need to talk to you, I need to understand."

"Understand what?" I said, with rising anger. "I thought you already understood everything. I'm a freak, remember? I'm a jinx. What do you want me to do, Tobias? Disappear?"

"Yes! Yes, disappear, go away, take the bad things with you. Just go, you're not wanted here."

"You really expect me to say yes, don't you? Sure, I'll pack my bags and leave, nice and quiet, and you can forget you ever knew me." I pushed away from the door to hover just before his bubble, and stared in at him through the shifting splotches of light. "Except, dear child, I don't make bad things. I'm not responsible for evil. I'll be gone soon anyway, but that's still not quick enough for you, is it? You don't want to see me die, right? That's what's bothering you. I'm going to die, dead, death, corpse, rot, and that's all you're worried about. Well, I will not go away, dear child, I will not go away at all."

"I'm not your child!" Tobias screamed, and clutched at his wrist-band. The nearest remote rushed

at me, cutting arms opened and straining. I spun, twisted, ducked under one metal arm and pushed myself into the doorway, and suddenly my mouth was filled with saltwater.

We both stared, horrified, at the cut and trailing hose that dangled from my mask, before I turned and fled into the building.

45

I rushed through the lobby, grabbing my hose from the mask. It was cut near the tanks, and could not help me; a river of air spilled and bubbled, rising toward the dark ceiling. I slapped the valve shut. I had to reach Mitsuyaga's room.

Gripped by a total, blinding panic, I kicked through the lobby and across the inner waiting room. My lungs burned and my ears thundered; I could not find the staircase. Light flooded the room behind me as Tobias entered, and I thought I heard him shouting through my terror, but I must have been wrong: why would Tobias shout about children at the bottom of the sea? I kicked, pushed, spun, frantic to avoid the metal killers behind me, frantic to find the stairwell, to get to the safety of the hidden room. I saw the staircase, finally, and rocketed for it, miscalculated, and crashed against the wall. A blinding agony flared through my shoulder, through my chest, exploded the air from my lungs, and the bitter seawater flooded in. I screamed into the ocean, refusing death with a total, silent cry of rejection.

A sharp pain burst in my skull, a wrench, a pull, and I found myself thrashing naked on a soft, dark floor. I clung wretchedly to the dark solidity, coughing, gagging, water pouring from nose and mouth. My throat and lungs ached, abraded, and the floor spun sickeningly below me. The shaking slowly flowed from me and away, leaving me alone in the blackness.

৫ 46 ৵৯

A passing of time, and my fingers worked at the soft coldness below me, my still-stinging eyes squinted into the darkness. I was . . . in my room? Yes. Yes. But how had I come here, to the hulking machines?

A painful wrenching of the head, doors in my mind ripped open—I had come by coming. I had the need to be here, and I was here. I sat, feeling my naked skin shrink from the cold, and I probed tentatively at the sore spots of my brain. Open doors; a simple jump from controlling the parts to controlling the whole, yes. But my fingers still sought confirmation from the floor below, my lungs from the chill, dry air. And here I was.

Carefully, then, I formed an image of the room's arch, held it steady, and touched the open spaces of my mind. Something shifted swiftly, and I found myself lying under the arch, feeling its curves along my hips. Back again to the hatch. Odd. Interesting.

Strength crept back to me; I formed an image of the stairwell, took a deep breath, shifted. Tobias' remotes floated through the room, trailing the emptiness of my discarded suit after them. Very quickly, then, to the entrance, before my air was exhausted. How different it felt, from the cold dryness of the room, from the still waters of the stairwell, this closeness to the heaving currents of the ocean. How different the sights, as though a series of quick cuts interrupted a sensum show. I peered through the mosses and plants and saw Tobias' bubble, but his back was turned to me. Tobias had tried to kill me. Tobias? Me? Tia? I did not wish to let him see me, and my lungs complained. Back to the room, then, leaving Tobias and my terror elsewhere. Oh, the Immortals can't do this, only I can, me, Tia. I sat upon a dark floor in a dark room and felt pleased, felt proud, patted myself upon the head and crowed.

Can I perceive through darkness? No, not simply by asking. Which door do I enter? What is its name? Where are the answers?

What are my eyes?

Cornea, iris, pupil, lens. Sclera, choroid, vitreous body, ciliary body. Retina. Optic nerve. So.

Sharpen this, here. Strengthen that, yes. And sensitize the other. A bare phosphorescence of the sea, a gleaming, and I change, touch, move. Dim shapes in the darkness of the room, differing shades of blackness. Oh, I am right, I am true, I am sufficient. I am good, better, best of all, me, Tia, I can do things they never dreamed of doing! Dance, sing, shift, shimmer—alone and complete at the bottom of the sea!

47

I would like, I think, some food. And something to drink. A little light would be nice. Perhaps some warmth, although I have adapted quite successfully, I think, to the cold. Fresh air. Let me not be greedy, though. A little at a time. Some food. And something to drink.

I rose gently through the clear blue waters below the bulk of the *Ilium*. Sleek ocean along my skin, cool satin flowing and folding about me running quicksilver through spreading hair and across eyes. The waters shifted and I spun, enfolded, protected, cradled, lady of the oceans, mistress of the seas. I gazed about me at dim, quivering shapes, wondered at their lack of detail. What is wrong here? I peered, squinted, felt a small passage of discomfort across my spine. Why can't I see clearly? With my mask I could—protect my eyes—function in air rather than in water. Oh—

I explored the secrets of my cells, secreted transparent eyelids below my opaque ones, refined them to handle the distortion of objects seen through water. The new lids slid into place as easily as though I had always had them, and my undersea kingdom leaped into focus. Oh, I am worthy, capable, powerful, right! Let the Immortals try that!

But I had not yet learned how to breathe the sea, and the room was three minutes behind me. I shifted to the waters below the *Ilium*'s diving well, pulled myself halfway to the lip and listened intently. Where are the Immortals? Shall I grow eye-stalks to peek over the edge into the mosaic hold? Are they waiting for me? I raised my head cautiously, peered about, then raised myself up and over the lip of the well.

The hold was empty and bright, too bright. I snicked back my new eyelids, narrowed my pupils until the light no longer pained me, sharpened my vision until I could count the individual rivets in the vaulted ceiling high above me, the small pores and lines of my hand, and was satisfied.

Padding to my locker, I irised it open and found it empty. Neither scrap of plastic nor shred of rubber, not an overlooked valve or screw. Forgotten so soon, then? Or gratefully discarded? No matter, for I had as gratefully discarded them. Not their tools, though. For these I must raid their supply hold, and cautiously. I had no wish to meet them on my way.

Ding, dong, the witch is dead! How gleefully they must have cleaned me out!

I remembered a bend in the corridor near the supply hold, sharp enough for concealment yet commanding a view of the corridor in each direction, a good place from which to search for Immortals. I carefully constructed a picture of the bend in my mind, then shifted confidently. But instead of an easy transition, I materialized in the corridor and some huge force flung me backwards, bounced me against the corridor's curving wall and left me sprawled on the

floor. A cry of pained surprise echoed from the other
side of the bend, and I glanced up to see Hart, flat on
his back, staring at me in shock. The cry became a yell
of terror as he scrambled to his feet and shot around
the bend, leaving the charts and maps he had carried
scattered behind him. I, equally frightened, shifted
immediately to the diving hold and slumped against
my empty locker, tried to calm the pounding of my
heart, the constriction of my chest. What in hell had
happened?

Simple physics, I assured myself once I had suffi-
ciently recovered. Two bodies, the same space, the
same time. Hart already occupied the space, I appeared, and the power of the universe enforcing its
laws threw us apart. Simple, and terrifying. I had no
wish to repeat the event.

Well, I knew enough empty and deserted places
about the *Ilium*. My cabin, too, contained a small
alcove, a place that would only by the remotest chance
be occupied, a place where I stored trivia. I shifted
cautiously, but my relief at arriving safely soon became puzzlement. My alcove was empty, my trivia
gone. I glanced about me, then stepped into the cabin.
Empty, stripped, bare. Where was my hammock? My
desk? My books? Had they consigned my belongings to
the deep in lieu of my body?

No matter. I didn't need the junk I had collected,
my world no longer encompassed a need for senti-
mental objects. It did, however, encompass a need for
food. I tapped the console and was relieved to find it
still operable. I ordered a plate of shrimp, a glass of
wine, made myself a chair from the wall and relaxed
while I ate and considered my next move.

It would be easier, I thought ruefully, if I could
make myself invisible, could step unseen about the
ship without running the risk of another universal
reprimand. I probed my brain, but that door was not
yet ready to be opened. In time, in time. And in the
meantime?

To the supply hold, obviously. One remote, well stocked, would meet most of my needs, but there were additional pieces of equipment that I wanted. To the galley for some food other than the remote's survival rations. Then back to my underwater room. With some care, I should be able to avoid a repeat of the corridor mishap. Avoid confined spaces. What if I were punched right through the side of the ship? Avoid crowded ones. Imagine arriving like a small explosion in the midst of one of Greville's lectures, scattering astounded Immortals right and left about me. I retracted the chair, placed plate and glass in the dispos, glanced at the room one last time and, picturing an empty corner of the supply hold, I shifted.

I snuck silently through the large chamber, assured myself that I was alone, then began assembling the equipment I wanted. The remote would have been refitted after the dive, would be waiting with the others in its niche along the inner wall of the diving well. But the additions would make life more comfortable: two powerpacks, an extra recycler, a miniature generator that ran on salt water and was barely enough, but enough, to recharge the powerpacks. The generator was another of Benito's toys; its run-off was potable water, and I remembered his glee as he demonstrated it to me that first time. Anything else? Yes, a homing signal to guide the remote from the *Ilium* to Mitsuyaga's building. I gathered the objects, oriented myself, shifted to my underwater room, and arrived with empty arms. I stared down stupidly, sharpened my sight, peered at the soft black floor. Nothing. Shifted to the supply hold and found the equipment piled chaotically on the floor.

I sat beside the cycler and considered. It couldn't be simply a question of tissue, blood, bone and nothing else, for I was stuffed with artificial parts and, I rapidly assured myself, all my plastic pipes and metal joints were still intact, still functioning. Why, then, could I not shift the equipment? The question was urgent, for without supplies I could not remain in the room. Without extra cyclers and powerpacks my time would be too limited, and there were things in the room I needed time to explore. Without the power-packs, the room was dead.

Calm, then. Logic. Deduction. The aliennesses of my body followed me because they were . . . assimilated? Accepted? Part of me? It sounded right. Because my mind accepted them as necessary to myself. That which I called Tia, called myself, encompassed certain portions of the universe. An invisible layer divided everything that was me from everything that was not me. But, perhaps, the invisible shield could be expanded.

I hefted the recycler, imagined a bubble of awareness enclosing both myself and it, and when I had the image firmly in mind I added the picture of the hatch room, shifted, stood in the soft blackness of my room with the cycler still in my grasp. Clever Tia, clever Tia. I placed the cycler on the floor, grinned, shifted, loaded my arms with the remaining equipment and shifted again. I deposited the booty on the floor, flickered to the building's entrance and pasted the homing signal to the wall, activated it, and returned to the diving hold.

Next to the galley. I shifted to a little-used storage chamber, checked about me, found Li missing, and cheerfully robbed his store of three bottles of wine, two loaves of his fresh-baked bread, a dozen assorted fruits, a slab of Argentine beef, and a sealing unit to keep the food fresh. On impulse I added half a round of cheese, some stasis packages of vegetables, and three fruit tarts, then shifted myself and my loot to the room.

And back again to the diving hold. It took only a moment to program the remote to the pulses of my homer, and I watched it slide through the clear waters and away.

Was there anything more for me here? Just curiosity,

and I could afford, I decided, to indulge it. My wants
were supplied and it took only some fraction of a second to go home again. Where were the Immortals? I
couldn't leave them, I decided, without a final glance.
And if the glance were of gloating and triumph, what
of it? I deserved to crow.

48

I shifted to the Museum, peered through one of the many arches along the sunlit chamber, found no one. But the quality of the light was wrong, something missing, and I stepped fully into the room. Every mirror was shattered, slivers and bands of glass lying broken amid the cracked display cases. Long jags of mirror hung precariously from the edges of the frames, reflecting my passing in distortion; the floor glistened with refracted light. I stood amazed, then picked my careful, barefoot way through the chaos. Why? Who? Why? Because of me, in some way; my displays were the most damaged, my discoveries all destroyed, and I did not understand. At the far end of the room I reached for the newest display, the pens found in the ruins of Hilo, and did not find them. The room was no longer mine, the work and skill and memories exorcised with fury; I glanced again and shifted to the engine room.

The generators thrummed deeply around me, powering the fields and services of the ship. Still scattered at the base of the broken generator were Benito's tools, forgotten amid the hulking bronze monsters. Or, perhaps, the Immortals had fastened superstitions on them, and they would lie forever on the polished floor, the only tombstone Benito would have. As, perhaps, the Museum would be mine? It seemed appropriate, and I walked carefully around the tools, climbed to the revolving platform, and stood above the ranks of dials and gauges.

Small, highly colored scenes flashed by me as I stood, my fingers brushing the cool plasteel of the control board. Benito hunched over the dials and buttons, manipulating the generators as the *Ilium* descended smoothly into the sea. Benito creating his toy, his sculpture, with microscopic precision. Benito flung over the naked side of the generator, dying to protect his ship as much as to protect those who sailed on her. Benito in orange wool.

Something dropped heavily on the floor, and I spun around to see Tobias frozen against the bulk of the dead generator, his eyes huge and staring from a newly pale face. Every muscle taut, fingers stiff and outspread, knees locked in fright. A large glassite voltmeter lay shattered at his feet.

Scared witless.

"Tobias," I said, grinned, stretched my hand toward him in sardonic greeting. He leaped backward, striking his shoulder against the generator, and the motion broke the seals of his voice.

"I killed you," he said harshly. "You're dead. I killed you. I brought your suit back, you're *dead!*"

"Don't you wish. Want to touch my arm, Tobias? I'm not even close to dead. Here, touch."

"Stay away from me!"

"Think I'm a ghost? You didn't hurt me at all, Tobias, not at all."

"That's what I told them. I said you'd killed yourself, that you stripped off your suit. They can't prove

you didn't. We had an argument because you wouldn't
obey orders, even Harkness' orders, and you got angry and killed yourself. You're dead. The remotes
have voice tapes, Greville has your suit. You're dead!"

"Yes? And everyone believed I'd kill myself because I was angry?" It seemed funny beyond words.
"Despite the cut airhoses? Despite the shut valve on
the tank? Do they believe you, Tobias?" I laughed.
"They send murderers to Australia, Tobias. Shall I
meet you in Australia? I'm not dead, Tobias. Here
—here." I moved toward him, reaching with my hand,
wanting to punish him with the touch of my warm
flesh. He danced nervously back from me.

"The Museum, Tobias, did you do that, too? Did
you?"

"It was *your* place," he cried. "In all the glass, in
all the mirrors! Tia, what kind of children do you
have?"

"You filthy little bastard," I said, brushing his
frozen face with my fingers.

"No!" he screamed. He dove to the floor, lifted the
laser torch from Benito's pile of tools, and leveled it at
me. His eyes were terrifyingly cold. This Immortal was
going to kill me—I'd never really believed it before. I
tried to shift but the panic blocked me; the doors of my
mind were closed tight.

"No, Tobias," I whispered. "Be sensible. They
might believe you, now. Let me go, Tobias. They'll
send you to Australia if you do this. Tobias?"

His eyes didn't change. "I'll be in Australia anyway," he said, in a voice devoid of any intonation. It
was like arguing with an implacably programmed machine, and I couldn't move for fear.

"Not here, Tobias. You'll blow up the ship, everyone will die. Not here."

His gaze flashed from me to the regiments of generators, and I leaped over the edge of the platform
and crouched, begging myself to shift. And couldn't.
Above me, Tobias bellowed.

I scurried toward the generators and ducked behind

the closest one, the one on which Benito had died.
Tobias screamed my name, and his feet pounded on
the metal deck. I ran, swerving through the bronze and
golden monsters, hearing the tell-tale slap of my bare
feet against the echoing deck. The shuttered door
gleamed dully on the far wall, in sight and out again as
I ducked and skidded and slid, and wished that I
could fly.

I slapped the palm-lock on the door as I bounced
against it, jumped out of sight beyond the generators
and, as the door irised open I leaped again, through
the gaping portal, and sprinted down the corridor. I
slid into a branching corridor, into another, into a
third, and slumped against the wall, panting, shaking,
unable to stop the panic. Tobias? I couldn't hear beyond the pounding in my ears, and every new-found
skill had fled from me.

My heel scraped against the wall and the sound sent
me bounding into the corridor. Tobias screamed in-
articulately, and the side of the corridor bubbled vis-
cously at the laser contact.

I dove up the lift-tube, knowing he couldn't fire for
another thirty seconds. The bar for the third level
rushed downwards, and I grabbed it, swung out of
the tube, and sprinted down the corridor toward the
wide balcony surrounding the well. I needed a floater, a
flyer, wings, anything, but there was nothing at all.
Tobias flew from the lift-tube and sent a beam of light
chasing across the emptiness of the well toward me. I
slipped on the tiles, skidded on my hip, smashed against
the balustrade, and spun off. Ahead of me, a section
of corridor hissed into slag.

I crouched and scuttled along the balcony and he
paced me, waiting for the laser to charge again. I
stared back at him, each glimpse punctuated by the
broadness of the balcony's supports.

"*Ti-a!*" he shouted, and his voice echoed. I
shuddered. It couldn't be Tobias, not that white and
staring face, the bulging eyes, the twisted mouth. *I'm*

the nightmare, I thought in confusion, as he shouted my name again.

At the corner the railing became solid, cutting my view. I paused, tense, knowing that his laser was charged again. I still couldn't shift, and my body felt slick with cold sweat.

"What's going on here?" the intercom barked. I glanced over the railing and saw Tobias staring in shock at the speaker. I dashed to the lift-tube, flew up the gleaming shaft, grabbed the bar at the top and catapulted onto the mosaic flight deck. Again I lost my footing and slid behind the hopper. I grabbed a strut and held tight, trying to catch my breath. The side of the hopper sizzled and I tore across the deck toward the minaret.

Voices shouted, and I could not tell whether they came from the intercom or not. It didn't matter, and they barely made sense.

"What is it? What—"

". . . laser! Stop! I command—"

"I told you it was here! I told you—"

"Stop them! Stop them!"

"Who? What?"

"*Tiiiiiii---aaaaa!*"

The staircase twisted, slippery, and I ran up it with Tobias one curve behind me. I ran faster, terrified of tripping, terrified of stopping, terrified of falling, terrified of slowing, and finally burst onto the topmost walk, the narrow ledge that girdled the minaret fifteen meters above the waterline. There was no exit, save for the staircase. No crevices, no niches, no place to hide. I could not stop myself from running, and ran all the way around the ledge until it brought me within sight of the staircase again, as Tobias jumped onto the ledge and saw me. I stopped and put my hand to the minaret's cold wall. He held the laser perfectly steady, the dim green ready-light glowing along its barrel. There was nowhere left to go.

"Tobias. Stop it. Please."

And Tobias' mouth moved, forming a word that I couldn't hear. He paced toward me slowly.

"It's not a game, Tobias. Stop now. Tobias?"

Still he advanced, and I didn't understand why he didn't simply kill me. I battered at the doors of my mind, my guts twisting with the effort to shift, to move, to leave, but the doors were locked and I could not find the key again. Footsteps sounded on the stairway, voices shouted on the deck below, and Tobias chewed his word inaudibly. His hand never shook.

"Tobias!" Jenny raced onto the ledge and froze, but his gaze on me didn't waver. The laser lifted and he sighted, carefully, his finger on the trigger.

"STOP!" I screamed with my mouth, with my mind, with my guts, with my soul. *STOP!*

And Tobias stopped.

His expression did not change as he toppled forward and lay still. One hand dangled over the drop to the flight deck. His finger relaxed from the trigger.

We approached him slowly, Jenny and I. I knelt, touched his neck, rolled him over. His lips twitched and I bent lower, straining to hear.

"Mother," Tobias said, and left me staring into clear and lifeless eyes. His chest, below my hand, emptied and was still. Jenny stood and, shocked and bewildered, I looked up at her.

"I tried to tell you," she said flatly. "He's as mortal as you are."

"But—" I said. "I'm not his—"

"It doesn't matter. You killed him." Jenny shuddered, sat on the deck, and stared with eyes as lifeless as Tobias' out across the sea.

49

I stood, staring at Jenny, then beyond her to where the other Immortals clustered at the top of the stairs. Harkness clutched the rail, knuckles white, white around the corners of his clenched jaws; Greville behind him, staring, his face almost as bleached as the dyed tufts of his hair. Hart, body shaking beyond control. Li. Lonnie. Paul, face scrubbed of any emotion at all, beautiful in his shock. And Jenny, completely lost now, her eyes reflecting the clarity of withdrawal. Slowly their attention shifted from the death to the doer, and I was impaled by their gaze.

"Please. I didn't mean . . . did you hear him . . . I didn't want . . ." But I *did* want. "He was going to kill. . . ." But *I* had killed. Had stopped him. Left him lying completely alone on the sunbaked ledge, the only other one like me, dead of my fraudulent superiority, of my panicked pride. I had murdered

Tobias. And had no weapon I could fling from myself
in disgust, for *I* had done it. All by myself.

"Please," I pleaded to the jury that could not ab-
solve me, and horror woke slowly in their eyes. I took
a step toward them and they backed away from me,
groping with their feet and still staring, seeing my guilt
fresh branded on my face. We moved in silence, across
the ledge, down the sun-drenched, winding staircase,
and I could no more move away from them than they
could come toward me. Down and down, leaving
Jenny and her dead lover alone at the crest of the
Ilium. How many people had I killed up there?

They clumped on the mosaic deck, moving as one
entity from me as I paced toward the edge of the
ship, toward the waters below. I turned when I
reached the rail, saw them huddle together by the
hopper and, high above, the spire of Jenny's body
etched against the blueness of the sky. In the limitless
stillness, the door in my mind swung open.

"I'm sorry," I whispered, and shifted down.

50

Hours passed, maybe days. The room hummed around me, warmth stole from the walls, air circulated, food sat untouched about the walls of the anteroom. I sat at the entrance to Mitsuyaga's kingdom, unable to move.

"Mother," he had said. And died. He was no child of mine; I had no children, could not have children. "He's as mortal as you are." As I? Dying? My head spun and I could not find the marrow of concentration, could not touch each thing in its place. "Mother," he said, after I killed him. Me? All by myself?

When I first met Tobias (sitting in the hold mending a rubber tube, and Greville wafting down the shaft followed by gold perfection: one is drawn to the beautiful and strange, a drawing neither of love nor hate, but simply of presence. Magnet and filings; one has to stare) he started and turned pale, eyes round, fingers stiff and open, and I retreated to sarcasm, thinking it the typical reaction, but more so. But—as mortal as I? Tobias? Is that why he had stayed, drawn by my destiny as I was shamed by his beauty? No child of mine, that golden boy; did he watch his future in myself? Is that what he meant? Why he hated?

A child crying in the veldt, a child moving tight and terrified through the streets of a dozen cities, fleeing from planet to planet and staring into mirrors for the claws of age . . . Tobias? But I was never as beautiful as he. Not I. And he was no child of mine.

I had never asked his age, never known it until he whispered it to me on the run, and I hadn't stopped to reason why.

"No, there's no one like me. Do you find that a relief?"

"I tried to tell you. He's as mortal as you are."

Jenny stared with eyes as empty as her lover's; how many people did I kill up there?

No, he was no child of mine. But he could have been; he might as well have been. There was no virtue in me.

I looked up, through the flocked silence of the room. And sighed. And stood. Too many questions, too much guilt. I could not rob Tobias' death of meaning by endless speculation, could not murder him twice. Beyond the room the sea pulsed, the moon moved through its cycles, the earth swung about the sun and the sun about the galaxy. For a purpose, for a purpose, and it was my task to find a purpose to this pain, to these deaths. Create a funeral rite of meaning.

A fish dies, and dying gives life to another fish, or to animals, or sinks to become part of the rich fertility of the ocean's floor. An ocean dies and gives birth to land in its passing. A cliff tumbles to the waves, and the ocean is both shrunken and enlarged. Continual process, and each death adds to the life of the cycle, each division multiplies, each subtraction adds. There is a harmony to this, neither life nor death uppermost, and it is the balance, the contrast, that gives each

shape its meaning. This, then, is what Lippencott's
Children lost. What I lost. The comfort of change, the
dignity of process.

He might as well have been my child. Let my payment for his life be the peril of my own. He should
have been my son.

I passed down the long room until I stood before
the dark bulk of Mitsuyaga's last, untested creation.
Touched the grey spot and the lump cracked in half,
the two sides moving ponderously aside to reveal, set
on a small black ledge within, a stoppered flask. Nothing else. No screen, no list of languages, no agglomeration of words. I took the flask in my hand, watching
the grey liquid move within, as thin and light as water. All it lacked was a label reading "Drink Me."

Behind me, a couch rose from the floor. I sat upon
it, flask held in my fingers. Felt no hesitations, no
expectations, no extremes. I unstoppered the flask,
lifted it, silently toasted Tobias, and drank the fluid.

I felt a profound shifting, as though the universe
had changed gears. I lay back on the couch, closed
my eyes, and let the empty bottle fall from my fingers
to the soft floor below.

The darkness behind my eyelids gave way to shape,
color, a movement of something just beyond the edge
of comprehension. I hesitated, finding no referent in
this constant, beguiling flow. Streamers of delight, ten-
drils of euphoria, sly vines of pleasure seeped from
the kaleidoscope and beckoned. And beyond, nothing.
To surrender to the flood was to slip forever into ecstasy, into the dance of nonbeing, away from what I
was, had been, would be, and the longing to merge
with the enchantment tore at me. But I searched for
meaning, not death, not ecstasy. Would not use Tobias' fate, or Benito's, or my own, simply to retreat
more elegantly from the question. I waited, torn and
patient, for meaning to arrive.

Slowly, then, the kaleidoscope was bounded by un-
definable walls. My perceptions sharpened and I saw
divisions within the swirling, the constants amid the

change. The pattern grew clearer, the manic dancing
became ordered, stable, almost set in its change. Reassured, I ventured into it.

This was immediately familiar, once into it. This
the expansion of my lungs, this the beating of my
heart, all the solid internalities. Thick and strong,
these cords and convolutions, binding the parts to one
whole. I reached for the brighter, lighter pulses of my
senses: sight, and the colors shifted and churned,
blazed and mellowed; sound, and great, complex
chords surrounded me, carillons pealed amid the high,
young voices of flutes. Smell, and I was besieged by
subtle fragrances that seeped through my entire being,
that blended and danced with the bells and colors.
And taste, and touch; I opened myself to the flood,
embraced, praised, danced with the dances of my
body. And moved on.

Here, a spinning galaxy. I entered and memories
inundated me—the desert house of my childhood, the
coolness of lizards on my palm, my mother's voice,
dead volcanoes rearing against an intense sky, packages of sweets stolen from my mother's lovers, the
burnt hole of Nevada buzzing on the air-shuttle's
counter, the caves of ice below the pole. The taste of
prickly-pears, trifle, apples toasted with cinnamon, the
scent of long summer days beside the sea, the touch of
pine and aspen.

Stars of sensation and novae of delight, but also the
burnt stars of fear, dark husks of shattered innocence,
black explosions of pain. Treatments. Hospitals. Dis-
trust. Hatred. Terror. Gaping holes in my life per-
meated with a sticky miasma of tears, and it came to
me that fifty years of self-pity is a criminal waste. I
entered the darkness.

Found it knit tight with the light, found the balance,
the Janus-faced opposites that created the meaning of
each extreme, an interconnection as delicate as the
precarious balance of life in a desert sink, as necessary
as sun and water. I listened, saw, touched, tasted, accepted the extremes and praised them. And moved.

Having surveyed the boundaries of my life, I reached toward the component pieces, turned them, nudged them, urged and pushed and settled and shaped until the dancers each moved to the same pulse, the same music, and the harmony was a creation of the dance, the dance the result of harmony. I felt the singing tensions of possibility within me, touched the essences of control, the nexus of change. I felt presence and power calling to me from beyond myself, and a new urgency suffused me. A single, simple step waited, but I hesitated, feeling the familiar and comforting sensations of my body, the totality of the cool, clean sweep of my mind, and, flooded with certainty, with sureness, I parted the strands, one by one, felt the last breath ease from my body, stepped from my husk, and rose.

❦ 51 ❧

I rise as an essence, as a wave moves, when every particle of water is different amid the force of the whole. Enchanted with my flowing, immersed in movement and curious, infinitely curious.

I scoop a passing tatter of the universe and make an organ for seeing—the galaxies stretch around me, clear, sharp, steady diamond chips tinted white or blue or red or yellow. Vast nebula mist in their courses, and spiral galaxies twist in a profusion of light. A handful of this, a shaping of so, and I eavesdrop on the sounds of the stars, the slow discourse of systems and the chittering of comets. I spin a web of sensation around me and spread myself among the stars, parsecs long, trailing auroras of ecstasy. Shift my sight and frolic with colors new and nameless, shift my senses and am happily inundated with novelties. I open, until I feel, over and under the all, a great and brooding calm. I reach for it and blaze with something more than ecstasy, something greater than peace. Stand awed and gaping at the heart of the universe until a gentle force sends me spinning again through stars, fired and alive. I dive, contracting myself to the size of electrons, expanding until my edges curl in on themselves at the boundaries of curving space. Streak through galaxies until I orbit a minor yellow sun, a minor blue-green planet, and look upon my home again.

The Americas, England, Europe, Asia. The Iberian Peninsula, the boot of Italy. Africa, Ceylon, India, Arabia. Indonesia, Australia, New Zealand. Pacific, Atlantic, Indian, Arctic, the blue jewel of the Mediterranean, the cold jewel of the Bering Sea. The sea of Okhotsk, Hudson Bay, the Gulf of St. Lawrence, the California sea stretching from the slopes of Shasta to the Sea of Cortez, and the necklace of the California Archipelago. Lake Victoria. Tung Ting. Tahoe. Baikal. Chad. Maracaibo. Titicaca. How can this tiny planet contain so much beauty? The Nile, a silver thread through blooming desert, Mississippi, Amazon, Yenisei, Mackenzie. Congo. Ob. Sao Francisco. Japura, Euphrates, Zambeisi. Ganges. The Susquehanna. The Western Bug. Strands of water, strands of light. The Sahara, Sturt, Dasht-i-Margo, Gila. Negev, Morrope, Olmos, Gibson. Kyzly Kum. Atacama. Ust'-Urt. Namid. Dasht-i-Kavir. The gleaming backbone of the Himalayas, the chain of the Rockies running from Arctic Circle to Equator. Blue of Leman amid the white of Alps. Grey-green brown-green blue-green agate of a planet, white-clasped between the Poles, mantled in cloud. I sit in the hollow of Vesuvius, slide laughing down the flanks of Shasta, shimmy invisible through the sunken alleys of Venice and emerge dripping at Dar es Salaam. Scatter and collect and stand above Gibraltar. Spread myself like a sail to catch the winds and belly majestically through the Sea of Panama and into the deep Pacific, scamper up the coast and find my redwood house, still and secure on its easterly cliff. The beachgrasses around it fill the air with the sharp clean lights of their lives, the succulents sing morphic songs, and birds hover, stalk, nest, die. I praise it, leap across and through the waters to a small room in a submerged city, see my body lying peacefully on a black ridge. I calm the movements of the machines, lift my body, and float it down the corridor, down the stairs, through the rooms and set it easily adrift on the solemn currents of the Pacific.

And, lastly, to the floating toyland of the *Ilium,* moving through the immensity of the sea.

The ship glows gently in the moonlight, and I absorb its beauty as I move through it, seeking, finding. Harkness has cried himself to sleep, lies snoring exhausted in his lover's arms while Hart stares at the unseen ceiling overhead and does not understand. Peace, Hart. Neither do I. Li moves amid piles of cheese in the galley, confusion assuaged by mounting trays of pastries. It's a lonely universe, Li. Take such comfort as you may. Lonnie lies sleeping in Paul's arms, drugged safely beyond the reach of dreams; her mind is a soft sponge that survives by absorbing, by filling to shape again. And Paul lies beside her, disturbed and confused, thinking vague, lustful thoughts about Australia. But the urgings of his sub-conscious are closed to him, and he knows not why he craves. Sleep, Paul.

Greville sits motionless beside Jenny's still form. Feeling responsible, feeling concerned, feeling horror, feeling pain. I am surprised at Greville's midnight thoughts, here where he has no image to maintain. And Jenny, mind closed tight, desperately blank, desperately awake. I move into her mind, into the strangeness of her thoughts that are, withal, so much like my own, and find small gaps, possibilities of comfort, chances of aid. Delicate, delicate—I reach to her and feel the tiniest flicker of response, and my world shivers with energy.

Above the mantle of cloud lie the infinite reaches of space, the calm and pulsing center of the universe, joy and light and peace. I reach to it briefly, then turn and bend myself toward Jenny's mind. I have work to do.

SCIENCE FICTION CLASSICS

Great reading for the present...and the future!

Science fiction is the rising genre in contemporary literature and no SF library is complete without these fine, enduring classics from Pocket Books.

Fantasy Novels from POCKET BOOKS